Return to dust

Dani Powell grew up in Brisbane and has lived in Mparntwe/ Alice Springs for the past twenty years. Her writing has been published in several literary journals and her location-based performances have been produced in and around Mparntwe/ Alice Springs as well as for ABC's Radio National. Formerly Community Producer of Big hART's *Ngapartji Ngapartji* project, Dani currently works with senior Ngaanyatjarra, Pitjantjatjara and Yankunytjatjara people on NPY Women's Council's 'Uti Kulintjaku' project. Dani has directed the NT Writers' Festival in Alice Springs since 2015. *Return to Dust* is her first full-length work of fiction.

Return to dust

DANI POWELL

First published in 2020 by
UWA Publishing
Crawley, Western Australia 6009
www.uwap.uwa.edu.au
UWAP is an imprint of UWA Publishing,
a division of The University of Western Australia.

ISBN: 978-1-76080-138-0
Design by tendeersigh
Cover images from Xmentoys (Shutterstock) and Bogomil Mihayliv and
Lysander Yuen (Unsplash Images).
Printed by McPherson's Printing Group

'And you will eat the plants of the field;
By the sweat of your face
You will eat bread,
Till you return to the ground,
Because from it you were taken;
For you are dust,
And to dust you shall return.'

Genesis 3:18–19

PROLOGUE

I am calling her Amber because amber is my favourite stone. In truth, it is not a stone at all. Technically, it is fossilised tree resin that has withstood all kinds of weather and woe, the likes of which would normally cause sap to disintegrate. Amber resists decay.

I am calling her Amber to give her something precious. To remind her of what the world has to offer. She knew this once, more keenly than most. But she has forgotten. I am hoping to remind her that the world's beauty isn't gone. That beauty exists inside things, sometimes trapped, often obscured.

I read once of a baby bird preserved in Burmese amber for 99 million years. Complete with thread-like feathers, claws and even soft tissue, intact around the eyelid and ear, the fossilised hatchling became the most complete known bird to be recovered from the Cretaceous period. It was poised, as if for hunting – body lifted, beak open, claws splayed, wings fanned – when it had been embalmed in honey-like syrup.

While amber has always been used for adornment, the earliest pieces of amber jewellery, according to archaeologists, were not exclusively worn for decoration. Amber was believed to possess magical qualities and appears to have been used in rituals. Neolithic people carved amber into figures and symbols, which were worn on the body as charms, or sometimes sewn into clothing. Amber beads have also been found in what appear to be sacrificial deposits, and in graves.

I am calling her Amber that her name might be worn as a charm, a talisman for her travels, tucked under her collar, or carried in her hem.

Amber has been found at hundreds of sites around the world, but the largest quantities are said to come from forty-million-year-old deposits in the eastern Baltic region. Baltic amber was called 'Freyja's tears' by the Norse. Freyja was a warrior goddess of Norse mythology, who married the god Óðr. There are many versions of this myth, but one of them goes that soon after they wed, Óðr disappeared. All feared he was dead. Freyja cried amber tears, or tears of gold, but refused to accept his death. She wrapped herself in a magical cloak made of falcon feathers that enabled her to fly and, bird-like, she searched the earth for him. Indeed, Óðr had not died but had been banished and lost at sea.

Similarly, the ancient Greeks named amber the 'tears of the Heliades', the Heliades being the daughters of the sun god Helios and Clymene. Their brother Phaëthon died after attempting to drive his father's chariot, which was in fact the sun, across the sky. The sisters mourned for four months, until their unrelenting grief transformed them into poplar trees. Their tears were turned to golden amber, or *ēlektron* in ancient Greek.

It is plausible to me that grief might do this – might turn a person to wood, their tears to stone. That a tear can trap old sorrows together with the new. But grief is no longer spoken of like this. Our language around grief has dried up. We choose words that mask or underplay it, that suck the sting out of it and make it benign. We do not speak of petrification, of grief turning people to calcareous or siliceous stone. We wait for things to be right again, for order to be returned, and expect the grieving to remain unchanged.

We have relegated mythology to a place of make-believe, and so deemed myths untrue. But the word 'myth', from the

Greek *mûthos*, simply means story, tale or narrative. Stories of how the world came into being, stories to explain humanity. Is a story less true if it departs from life? Or if it compresses time or characters to impart its truth?

I am calling her Amber because some of her story is mine, and some is not. I have reached for fiction when the things that happened became too difficult to return to, or retell. And I have turned myself into Amber, because that, in truth, is what happened to me.

Begin Again

From the sky, the country is a sea, a swirling petrified sea. A stilled life of embryonic waves and calm, of endless cradles and peaks. Cloud shadows drift like ghosts, becoming and unbecoming, seemingly unconcerned. Vegetation appears in scalloped patterns, dark scalds on a red sea floor, which is sometimes pink, sometimes purple or bruised blue, beneath scattered skylight.

This is how Amber can live here, so far from the coast. She cannot plunge into its earthy mouth like she can in the open ocean, but she can rest her eyes upon it. She can throw her thoughts into this landlocked country and let them be tossed and turned by something outside herself. She can cast her questions into it, and sometimes reel things in.

'It's like a painting,' says the woman in the seat in front of her, as if to the man beside her, but he is absorbed in a movie, headset fixed to his ears. She nudges him. He lifts a headphone away from one ear and she repeats herself. But something of the wonder expressed the first time is sapped by the repetition. 'I said, it's like a painting.' He leans across her, towards the window. 'It's getting pretty red out there,' he says. Then, as if counting an appropriate measure of time, he withdraws, shuts the headphone back over his ear and returns to his screen.

As they begin their descent, Amber starts to recognise the markers on a map that is familiar. The shimmering silver roofs of outlying settlements. The single ruled line of a tangerine road. Swathes of creamy, coarse-grained sand that snake across the country, and sometimes collide. A year ago the rivers were in flow. The country was green. Now they lie empty, waiting to be animated by the next good rain.

She has missed this country, this palette of colours. The red dust, the dirt roads, the on and on of it. The ground so solid, the sky so sure. Now the ranges appear, like ancient beasts in slumber. You can follow a single spine from east to west, in a line broken only by gaps and gorges. Three hundred million years ago they were as high as the Himalayas. It is hard to conceive that what is visible of these ranges is only the eroded remains. It is a cliché to describe this landscape as ancient, but age is what imbues it with such grandeur. The distant past is carried in the country, like memory.

When finally the town comes into view, it might be an island, adrift from the mainland, surrounded by an archipelago of Aboriginal communities and homelands. Another country, out of the minds of most. It is almost as if it had vanished in her absence, sunk beneath the waves, so that it is somewhat of a surprise to find it here upon her return. But it is as close as she's ever come to feeling at home in a place. Which is strange, given her birthplace is thousands of miles away.

But from that very first night of her arrival, ten years ago, when she climbed the hill behind the house in the late afternoon and looked out across the townscape, with the ranges reigning behind, the sky ringing blue, she'd felt a sense of coming home that made no sense. She wondered at first if it might have been the physicality of the landscape, which bore some likeness to the drought-ridden country where she grew up. Where the foliage was, for the most part, scanty and scrubby, with trees dispersed, mostly lining creeks and rivers; where water was often absent. And sepia paddocks littered with the bones of fallen beasts. Cattle stations and cleared land. Gates and grids and broken fences.

But, at the same time, this country was new to her. The rocky hills and foothills, the ranges that rolled out of town in bands of mauve and blue. The sandy soil and clay that made for resilient plants, like saltbush and mulga, that made it hard to grow things. The absence of moisture in the air.

Perhaps she'd been broad-brushing when she first arrived – grasping for the familiar, glossing over the detail, clustering together the known to counter the *terra incognita*. For the more she stayed, the stronger the lens, the more this country distinguished itself from anywhere else.

Perhaps the most particular difference was that, from the outset, she felt like she'd arrived in a foreign country. There was the immediate sense that it was somebody else's home. This was true of the whole of the continent, of course, but elsewhere you could avoid thinking about it. Here the people who belonged to the country were present. And this gave rise to an immediate tension for Amber, the conflict of feeling such a strong sense of home at the same time as being an outsider. It couldn't easily be resolved, and created for her a kind of push-pull relationship with the place.

But there was a kind of romance surrounding this fabled frontier town, in the middle of the desert, where the wind blows in. She'd hoped, in leaving a year ago, that she might be through with it. That it might fade for her, then dissolve forever. Yet here she is again, driven by the need to come home, hoping home will be enough. Soon she will be swept back into its current and things will be reversed, with the outside world becoming remote. And she can begin again.

SHALLOW NEST

There were plenty of people she could have asked for a lift, but she decided to catch the bus. She wasn't ready for conversation, for questions. She wanted to slip in silently and get her bearings. Tomorrow she will be gone again. For a few weeks, at least. After that, if she wishes, she can have a proper homecoming.

The strip of road between the airport and the town provides a prologue to the town proper. A motley line of gums spaced at semi-regular intervals on either side creates a kind of stark outback avenue, ushering people in from both the airport and the road from the south. Intermittent buildings, set back from the road, are plotted along the way. The boarding school for bush kids, run by the Lutheran church; an abandoned movie drive-in site, with its lonely concrete screen still standing in a prickly paddock; the aged-care home on the other side; and the cemetery hidden behind a band of low foliage. How many times has she passed these buildings but barely looked at them? The eyes are drawn ahead, past the rubbish tip, towards the ranges. And, soon, to the slim gap between them, through which you must pass to enter the town.

When she first came here, she heard stories that the southern rock face of this gap had been blasted by dynamite in the late 1920s, to make a level passage for the railroad track and the parallel road beneath it. Later she would learn it was a sacred site known as Ntaripe to the Arrernte people. Before the road, before the railway, Aboriginal women and children were forbidden to pass through. They could cross at a saddle a short distance east. The two stories sat in disharmony, unreconcilable, like so many others she would hear in the following years.

As the shuttle bus rolls in, people saunter along the edge of the highway, making their way from the outer camps into town. Just before the gap, a young mother pushes a battered stroller with a toddler twisting out of it. As she hurries along, the mother keeps turning to look back. The child is not strapped in, and as she arches her back, it looks as if she might at any minute topple out onto the narrow concrete footpath. A few metres back, a man appears to be calling to them, throwing an arm to the sky, one finger pointed. Amber watches him as the bus passes, trying to read the situation. But the bus pushes on, is funneled through the gap, and she soon loses sight of them.

They swing around the roundabout and turn onto the road that follows the river. A few blocks down, Amber leans forward to look through the front gates of the town camp, where she used to work, hoping to catch a glimpse of someone. There is the little building where she spent her days; its doors are shut, and there's no one around. A few people mill in front of a fire at the side of one of the houses. But the bus flies by too fast and the camp blurs.

When she worked here, the people, mostly women and young children, would drift over from the surrounding houses as soon as she opened up the community centre. Together they would cook toast, make cups of tea, tell her about the things that had transpired through the night. Of the chaos of the camp on nights of heavy drinking, when cars crashed through fences and smashed into houses. Or the music that throbbed all night, keeping everyone from sleep. Many times she felt she couldn't bear to hear another story of broken houses and broken bodies. Or to be the one who could leave at the end of the day. But they also told her how, on still nights, they would drag their beds outside and sleep beneath the stars. On those nights they would sometimes piece together stories told by their grandparents, describing a world that, in so short a time, seemed so far gone.

Winter mornings and the wind would sweep down from the hills, tackling rubbish bins to the ground that spewed their insides out, making a feast for camp dogs and a mess across the camp. Washing draped along fences to dry was often strewn across the ground. In the daytime the little community house filled up with people painting, cooking, laughing. In winter the women made small fires outside in the afternoon, when the wind had dropped. They'd sit together in the sun, searing holes through inernte, the brilliant red seeds of the batwing coral. Sometimes they used broken wire coat hangers heated in the fire to pierce the seeds. They would thread them with elastic to make necklaces and bracelets to sell to the tourist shops in town. In the old days they used hair.

The smell of burnt seeds and the warmth of those winter afternoons come to her now as the bus crosses the ephemeral river. Kids weaving around the dusty camp on second-hand bikes they'd fixed through a community outreach project, calling out, laughing, while in the circles of women conversation trickled. It was just like this, leaving the camp in the late afternoons, as people sauntered out of houses, sat down in circles, as cooking fires started up. Only to go home to the flat where she lived alone, just ten minutes away. The absurdity of it. The relief of it. The indulgence of it. The cleanliness of it. The loneliness of it. She feels it all again.

There is no one home when Amber arrives. Ruth has left the key under an old stone pot on the verandah, spilling with a straggly, purple-leaved succulent. The flat is empty, almost as Amber had left it. Ruth had held off renting it out in her absence, hoping she'd return. She had offered it instead to Andrew to use as an art studio during the day. But he'd stopped coming about six months ago, when he became too ill. Ruth had helped him move his things out. She hadn't got around to renting it out again, she said, and hoped Amber would return before she had to.

From far away, Amber had imagined it airing out, relinquishing the dog spirit and the sadness of that year. Her dog's death was the last thing. Without her, there was nothing to bring her home. And nothing to do but leave, it seemed. To let the wind blow in and sweep the sadness out. Let the place sit quiet and lonely for a time. And here it is, her little flat, wrung out by the wind and renewed. But how to relinquish the sadness in herself?

Soon after she came to live here, her brother sent a series of images of an abandoned mining town in Namibia, slowly being reclaimed by the desert. Sand had swept through open doors and seeped through broken windows, inundating the houses and turning the outside in; so that soon interiors became windswept landscapes, with kitchens, bedrooms, bathrooms half-subsumed. Sand spilled from one room to another, pouring down passageways like glacial rivers and settling in corners in sloping dunes.

She looks for traces of habitation but there are none, no leavings from the artist. But somehow the space feels changed. It has been painted. Gone are the peach-coloured walls she had grown accustomed to. The newly painted white walls and ceiling make the little two-roomed flat look larger than she remembers, luminous. With the curtains drawn, the winter sun spilling across the slate, she feels something flash so fast through her she can't quite follow it. A streak of sadness mixed with relief that the little place she'd etched in the world like a shallow nest was still waiting for her, intact. The act of kindness by her friend, not only to keep a place for her but to make it new again.

Amber goes out to the shed, where her boxes are stored. Immediately she begins brushing the film of dust from each of them with an old T-shirt before carrying them inside. Before long, her clothes are streaked with dust and cobwebs. She begins stacking boxes by the window in the main room, but soon tires of it. She sits on the slate, cold against her skin, before these towers of her belongings. Does she really need any of this?

Then she goes back out to the shed and climbs over the furniture, shifting more boxes to extract her old brown cardboard suitcase. She takes it inside and clicks the metal catches open. Her brother's artworks are bound in bubble wrap, as she left them. She starts to tear off the tape, ripping the plastic back in strips as she does. Then she stops. Sees her hands shaking. Feels the breathlessness in her body. *Slow down, slow down.* She bandages the artworks up again and tucks them back into the suitcase, snapping the locks shut. Still too soon.

Seeing Andrew

It is the afternoon light that draws her outside. A honey-coloured light that lifts the ordinary, or gives it grace. A winter's light. Over the fence, two magnificent red gums tower and taper towards the sky, with trunks as smooth as naked skin, pearly in the western light. Should she go and visit Andrew now or wait until she gets back? She'll only be away for two weeks. Perhaps she'll just go for a walk. Maybe she can drop in.

There is a small window of time to be savoured upon returning to a place you know well. When your senses are keener, sharpened by absence. Soon enough you will begin to merge again with your surrounds, and myopia will creep back in. As Amber walks, she appreciates anew the details of the place she'd left last year. She takes the lane behind the flat and follows the fence line – a patchwork of cobbled-together strips of corrugated iron and steel, preventing passers-by from peering in or wandering into backyards. But gaps between fence posts and gates left ajar provide small snapshots of life and how it is lived here. Open fires in shallow burrows of sand; strips of faded shade cloth stretched over garden beds; sheds, caravans, water tanks. The laneways that lace behind the streets in this part of town were once used for the truck to empty the outdoor toilets through small hatches in their back walls. Now they were rarely used, sometimes as walkways and bike paths and access points for properties, not much more. Elsewhere such tracts of land might be sought-after real estate, but here people have so much space the laneways were easily overlooked.

Some houses had lawns, watered diligently throughout the summer. But most backyards were a mix of sand and dirt and rocks, planted out with native trees and shrubs. Many people had fruit trees. In summer the mulberry trees grew massive, their branches draping over back fences, dripping with fruit. Kids skidded up the laneways on bikes, stopping to gorge on these offerings, before returning home with dark purple stains on their hands and faces and feet. You could sometimes look up the lanes and see only legs protruding, as groups of people disappeared into the mess of leafy branches.

At this time of year oranges, lemons, grapefruit, limes, cumquats adorn the trees, burning brilliance into an otherwise faded palette. Only a few doors up from her flat, a magnificent lemon tree looms over the back fence, crowded with fruit. You could climb the rusted steel rungs of the locked gate and pick lemons, with a quick twist of the stem. This evening the laneway is speckled with fruit, like fallen stars. Perhaps someone had shaken the tree. Delighted, she bends to inspect them, one by one, and gleans the fruit not yet rotted. She will take them for Andrew.

At the end of the laneway she turns to follow the dirt storm drain that diverts water away from the suburb and towards the river. Mostly dry, it carves a physical border between the street grid and the bush. She crosses over and, when she can, takes a dirt track towards the hill.

This is what she loves most about this town. This place of crumbling edges, where buildings, houses, blocks of land peter out into bushland all around. So that, one minute, you are treading footpaths, passing houses in orderly rows along strips arranged by street name, as in any other town or city; the next, you are traipsing along any one of the seemingly endless dirt tracks that carry you into the foothills, lure you along dried up tributaries and take you out and out, as the town dissolves in the dust of its own wake. Before you know it, you have stumbled across time and space.

Everything here, it seems, is constantly crumbling. House paint peels and flakes like winter skin. Timber splits. Things left outside deteriorate with time. Vegetables wither in the garden, waiting for rain. Washing is bleached on the clothesline. You put your dark colours out to dry at night to save them from the beastly sun that, by its glare, can suck the colour out of clothing and leave it haggard in so short a time. Here people constantly sweep out the dust. Brooms in hand, they fight to preserve the arbitrary boundary between outside and in, while in their daydreams they easily imagine a town returned to dust, should they let down their guards and leave it be.

All things domestic brace themselves against decay, hold themselves together against the barrage of the elements. The dry, the freezing winter nights. The sun, the sun, the sun. As do those who've come from someplace else to settle here. They shield their shoulders against the burn of sun; shade their faces from the summer rays. The soles of their feet form fissures, like the maps of the tracks and dry creek beds that thread through this inland country.

Amber doesn't have time to go off track this evening. She heads west towards the hill. These days, the little hill is cloaked in a blanket of buffel, a pasture grass introduced to keep the dust down, now smothering most of the central desert. To the exclusion of native grasses. To the extent that people now coming here think it *is* a native grass. Now only patches of orange rock protrude, like skinned knees in the overgrown grass, crisp and dry as hay.

It is one of a series of small hills that hold fast across the suburbs – even in the heart of the business zone – unkempt and seemingly unruffled by the commerce carrying on around them. Their presence is a constant reminder that, despite its growth, here the land still looms larger than the town. Despite settlement, the country holds its own.

Andrew's house is opposite the hill, on the edge of the drain. She hesitates for a moment at the front fence. The house seems quiet, shut up. It was unthinkable to imagine him sick. Of all the people she knew, he was one of the most vibrant, the most alive. He must have been ill before she went away. But he didn't say anything. He kept it to himself. She doesn't want to see him like this. She braces, clutches the loose lemons against her heart, then pushes the steel gate open, which lets out a low wail.

Wind chimes tinkle on the verandah. The front door is slightly ajar. She nudges it open. The inside stillness is that of a house with a sleeping baby. She calls out, softly. 'Hello?'

'Amber?'

'It's me.'

'Come on in,' he sings playfully.

She smiles, relieved. What had she expected – that the illness had taken his humour away?

She enters the house. It is like walking through an art gallery after hours, though somewhat more cluttered. Drawings and paintings adorn the whitewashed walls, watercolours and prints and bold acrylics in the signature styles of central desert art; lithographs, linocuts and etchings made by friends and fellow artists. Andrew's own medium was mostly sculpture, fashioning art from things he'd salvaged. Sculptures made of metal and timber and chiselled stone stand like sentinels in the corners of the room, while shelves are filled with small clay objects and rusted wire wrought into animal forms.

When she first came here, she was taken aback by the likeness to her brother's house. For as long as Amber can remember, her brother collected things, which he curated and catalogued with meticulous care. Mostly things from the natural world. Insects pinned to boards, dehydrated plants material packed into their grandfather's cigar boxes, strips of fungi like orange peel stored in the drawers of his cupboard. (He'd stuffed his clothes into two tiny underwear drawers to make room.) Every surface in the room they shared was soon transformed into a showcase for one specimen or another. Under the bunk bed, drawers filled with insects, spiders, skeletons, feathers and stones – all displayed in neat and narrow rows, labelled and dated with small squares of white card. As she grew up, a museum grew around her.

They'd go for walks with their mother on the cattle station where they first lived, and pick through the old rubbish tips. They'd bring home old irons they used as doorstops, horseshoes they hung over doors, branding irons, butter churns and washing tubs. Old bottles lined their windowsills, mottled with thread-like webs of earth – medicine bottles, beer bottles, spirits, tonics, colognes. Bottles embossed with brand names you could read with your fingertips. Green bottles, blue bottles, amber bottles, clear. Bottles that burned the light of the afternoon sun.

Many of these objects made it through their childhood and ended up in her brother's house. She'd kept some too, but she'd moved so many times it was hard to hold onto things. Her brother never stopped collecting. Collecting and drawing the things he'd found. So that, like Andrew, his house was a temple of beautiful things, each with a story.

How strange to find things 'the same as ever' in Andrew's house. They betray the scene in the bedroom, where her friend is propped up, bolstered by an ample stack of pillows. More like a sketch of her friend: his gaunt face, all bone and shadow. She is careful not to show her shock. The lemons spill onto the bed as she reaches to embrace him. His cheeks are warm from the gas heater at his bedside, his breath stale. The truth of his body had been masked by the shape of the flannelette pyjamas, so that it is another shock when Amber leans in and senses the cloth caving in, disclosing his bony frame. She feels herself recoil and hopes he doesn't feel it. She will not cry. Not in front of him.

'So your mother's looking after you?' She'd heard this from Ruth.

'My dear mother's been looking after me,' he says. 'Oh, and there's the roster. All these dear friends have been making the most delicious meals.'

'That's nice. Maybe I can get my name on that roster.'

'Yes, it's funny. Often they don't come in. I suppose they think I'm sleeping. So they leave these meals on the front verandah, like little offerings to the gods. And Mum brings them in before the local dogs get to them.'

'Mistaking them for little offerings to the dogs, of course.'

He smiles. She can still make him smile.

'Sometimes they leave little notes, which is sweet.'

Amber thinks how she'd hesitated at the front gate. She tells herself she didn't want to disturb him, to intrude, to burden him with the need to be social. But that wasn't it.

'But you'd like them to come in?'

'It gets a bit lonely sometimes.' He sighs. 'But then I *am* often sleeping and don't want to be disturbed!'

He laughs, just his plain old Andrew laugh. As if the man before her wasn't a skeleton at all. As if nothing had changed.

'We'll have to get one of those Do Not Disturb signs from the hospital, for your front door. Or we could make one with some other options on it, like Please Come In.'

'Please, *Please* Come In.'

'And Bring Vanilla Slice from the Trattoria.'

'Yes please! Let's get some humour back into this.'

'Where is she now, your mum?' she asks, thinking about the loneliness.

'Oh, she's out and about somewhere. Maybe visiting next door, or gone for a walk. She might have even gone to a movie with one of her new friends. She's a busy lady. She loves it here. Which is ironic, because before this all happened, I could hardly get her to come. Twice she came – *twice*, in twenty-five years!'

'It's expensive from Sydney, I suppose.'

'Rubbish. It would have been Dad stopping her. He expects his children to visit *him*. It's our punishment for moving so far away. Anyway, I think she's glad to get away from him. Death gives us good reason to do things.'

There it was. Death. Just dropped in, like that. Unannounced and unclothed – it was shocking. Andrew sees her surprise and goes to speak, but Amber flies into the open space with words.

'Sorry I didn't come back earlier. I wasn't ready, you know, to be here.' She can hear how selfish this sounds, but it's complicated and she doesn't want to reel off excuses either.

'Well, you're here now,' he says. 'That's all that matters.'

'Almost,' she hesitates. 'I'm off tomorrow. Emma contacted me to see if I could help her out with a school holiday project in Tjiwa.'

'Oh.' He pulls a sad face and Amber wonders why she didn't make more time before going away. More time for him. She thinks of the message he left on her phone over a month ago:

If I asked Amber to come back, would she? But she couldn't, not then. She wrote him a postcard: 'Not yet, but soon.' The truth is he gave her reason to return, a reminder of the things she still had here.

'It's only two weeks. Then I'll be back.'

'Good,' he says. 'Because I've got a job for you.'

It hadn't occurred to her there was a particular reason he'd asked her to come back. They'd spoken once or twice on the phone but he'd played things down, in the way he did. He'd given no sense of the severity of things. It was only when Amber spoke to Ruth about coming back to the flat that she learned of his rapid deterioration.

'I thought, given your creative streak, you could help me plan the funeral.'

'Me?' Amber blurts out, with a thin laugh. She is not so much surprised to be asked for help but to realise where he's at with it all. She doesn't want to be talking about his funeral, let alone preparing for it.

'My mother won't have a bar of it. I don't have a partner. So I was thinking, who could I ask?' He stops when he realises she hasn't spoken a word. 'Come on, it'll be fun!'

How can she say no?

'I'd like to be buried like my dog was buried. But I don't think that's allowed.'

Andrew's dog had been bitten by a snake a few years ago. It died that same day. A few friends went with him to the clay pans just south of town. It was the place he used to go to paint. All the while, his dog would dig out shallow burrows nearby, discarding branches and broken sticks beneath the mulga, then lay down in what Andrew came to call 'dog nests' while he worked. He painted these nests in time. When his painting companion died, he wanted to take her back to the place she loved. So he bundled her in a blanket in the back of the car and they'd driven out at the close of day, to find a burial spot.

They'd skirted the rim of the pans – now a series of shallow, empty plates – until they'd come to a grove of she-oaks. It hadn't rained in a long time and the ground was hard as bone. They'd chipped away with mattocks and shovels until they had enough depth for the body. They'd covered the site with heavy stones and crisscrossed branches to shield it from birds and prevent it from being dug up by wild dogs. It had gone on for some time, this silent vigil of placing rocks and branches. Then, in the stillness, they'd stood by the grave and tried to console their friend with stories they remembered about his dog.

But Andrew was not consolable. He stayed long after they left. Until the claypans appeared like flaky pink pie crusts in the moonlight, and the ranges blackened along the horizon, like the burnt edges of the coming night. Later, he told Amber that he'd buried nothing here prior to this, nothing that was *his*. 'All the things I've lost I seem to have lost to the dry air,' he'd said. The interment of his beloved dog had brought him to believe that burial binds us to place. After he buried her, he could claim this place as home.

So Amber knows what Andrew wants: to be dug directly into the earth, with no coffin to create a boundary between his body and the country.

'I think you have to be buried in a cemetery,' she says. 'In a casket of some kind. Unless you're cremated. Then you can be scattered anywhere, I suppose.'

'Well, whatever. But they're not flying my body back to Sydney.' It's the first time she's heard irritation in his voice. 'That's what my family will want to do. That's why I need to have something in place. So I can have what *I* want.'

Whether he senses her restlessness or whether it is his own agitation around the subject that makes him stop she is not sure, but she is relieved that he does. She isn't ready for this.

'Anyway, we can talk about it more when you get back,' he concludes. 'Two weeks, you said?'

'Yes,' she says. 'Let's leave it til I get back.'

As she passes through the house, it feels like she is being carried on a wave of sadness, yet to break. Everything in place in Andrew's house, untelling. All the beautiful things, collected, created, curated. All the effort. Even the world's turning, at times like this, feels like a deceit. Her need to get out of here becomes urgent. When she reaches the street, she gasps in air and wonders if she had actually been holding her breath.

It is so hard to fathom. She thinks of the last time she saw him, not long before she'd left. He was squatted on the front porch, tinkering away at something, when she passed. 'What are you up to?' she'd called over the fence.

'A pinhole.' Then, standing, he'd held up two pieces of card. 'A pinhole projector.'

He might have been announcing an act on stage, the way he'd pronounced the title of his creation, elevating the status of what appeared to be two squares of cardboard. But that was Andrew. Closer, she saw that he was indeed holding up two pieces of cardboard. It was a way to watch the solar eclipse safely, he'd explained, which was apparently happening the next day. Amber was charmed not only by the simplicity of the instrument but by Andrew's childlike absorption in its construction. It was something she'd forgotten. The absorption of play. She envied his ability to hold onto it.

He asked if she'd like to accompany him the next morning to watch the eclipse. So she'd gone with him at dawn, with a thermos of hot tea and the two squares of cardboard, one with a tiny pinprick that would be their viewing hole, the other a projection screen. They drove east to the foot of the nearest hill, then left the car and climbed in the first light, the summer sun already warm on their backs.

From the top of the hill the land fell away on all sides, stretching out towards the ranges in a series of small blunt peaks. They'd sat in quiet and shadow as the infant day reverted to temporary darkness, and delighted at the small silhouette of moon captured by this most primitive of tools. A new moon, made visible only by the eclipse. And she told him how, as children, she and her brother used to cup their palms under the moon and tell each other they were holding it in their hands, triumphant to have brought the cosmos closer, or perhaps made it seem less vast.

The moon comes up as Amber walks home and she feels a chill in the air. She hurries through the streets, thinking of what he'd said. Did he think two weeks too long a time, if he needed her to help with all of this? Then she wonders if it *is* too late. Why hadn't she come earlier, when he'd asked? Because we think we have all the time in the world, that's why. Grief heaves like a monstrous wave inside her chest.

Back at home she gathers what broken branches and sticks she can find from around the yard to make a fire. She smiles to see the remnants of previous fires still visible. No fireplace as such, just a circle where the sand is discoloured by powdery grey ash, a few crumbs of coal. She scrapes out a shallow bowl with her bare hands. The grainy sand against her skin feels strange, foreign. How easy it is in the city to be always at a distance from nature. Never touching the earth. The night is cold but the fire soon brings warmth. She shuffles close and watches as the stars press through the darkness. She is home.

THE SHADOW OF DEATH

It is early when she slips back out of town through the gap, silent as a silk thread through a needle's eye. On both sides the ranges still seem to be sleeping. Their presence offers a calm that is hard to describe. Perhaps it comes from stillness, from sheer mass, from age. She watches as they slide into the distance in the rear-vision mirror, then soon become a band of pastel blue, surreal against the pink tint of the morning sky.

To pass through the gap in the ranges is to enter another time, somehow altered or stretched so it starts to become difficult to keep. For three hours or so she hurtles down the highway before she turns off the bitumen and onto the dirt road. Now she feels the same sense of exhilaration she had when she first came to this country all those years ago, and each time after that.

Her first job was ferrying people to and from remote desert communities for respite, taking provisions like new swags to the elderly or sick. It was a strange job for one with little four-wheel drive experience, let alone any knowledge of the culture of the people who lived here. But it gave her the chance to cross country otherwise out of bounds, and to feel that in doing so she was being of some use. Those first trips had felt something like swimming out to sea as a child. Once she'd entered the saltwater, she'd wanted to go deeper and deeper. So swept away was she by this new land that she'd wanted nothing less than full immersion – to be on the backroads, the roads less travelled, entering *parts unknown*.

Before coming to the desert, Amber had no notion of this web of unsealed roads that track through the core of the continent, that sweep you along like tugging currents, that puncture your tyres and tip you over the moment your attention slips. Of the dirt tracks that trail off to homelands, to bores; some were hunting tracks that petered out after some distance, seeming to lead to nowhere.

In the *Jacaranda Atlas* they used at school, the desert appeared like an amorphous tea stain that spilled across the middle of the map. It wasn't until she decided to drive to the centre of the country that she studied it more closely. Not that you really needed a roadmap to find your way to the centre. A single highway shoots straight up the middle of the country. But she had to work out where to stop, where to fuel up, where to sleep. It was only then, once she had the map in her hands, that Amber had any sense of the magnitude of the desert, let alone the detail. She'd followed with her finger the roads and rivers, noting the names of gorges, gaps, cattle stations, wells. But the monochromatic pigment of the map kept the country flat and featureless.

Like any place, to come into it is to zoom in on the detail and definition – the contours, the landforms, the changing vegetation. But there is something else, signposted by this maze of unmapped roads only discovered when you leave the highway. A world unto itself. These roads are the webbing between a network of Aboriginal communities pulsing across the country, like low-burning campfires. Settlements that were once missions or ration stations or, later, homelands. Places she would come to know. People whose lives would cross her own.

By daylight there are signposts. Bearings given by place names, painted on the propped-up bonnets of dismembered cars, or by anecdotal directions. 'You'll see a forty-four-gallon drum on its side. Turn left.' 'There's two roads. Take the second. Then veer left when the road splits.' Some of these directions had been translated into mud maps for her over the years – scrawled on serviettes, in notebooks or on ripped-off corners of cardboard boxes. Without legends or keys, they'd become incomplete maps, indecipherable archives. But Amber has kept them all, these hand-drawn maps, as records of her road journeys. She loves the way place can be encoded in the simplest lines and drawings, pressed into paper, folded and contained. And how it can be remembered, so viscerally, once a map is opened again, transporting her back to places and times she might have otherwise lost.

There is little chance of getting truly lost. Most of the time she carries a GPS in the glovebox. Strange to think we can locate ourselves in the vastness by satellite. The old people would laugh. They would say, 'We don't need GPS. We got that GPS in our head.'

For hours, Amber crosses grasslands – flat, open country flecked with low shrubs, grasses, dispersed trees. Mostly acacias and eucalypts, twisting towards the porcelain sky. So solitary, these trees, so sparsely set, they seem like lonely figures travelling across the country. She thinks of her boxes, stacked by the wall in the flat, and is glad to be unencumbered. Nothing between her and the country but the carapace of the car.

Soon the road begins to rise and fall, carrying her across sand dunes, then through a forest of desert oaks – trunks black as burnt matchsticks, leaves sharp as needles yet somehow soft, weeping. Then on and on until a small huddle of hills butts up against the road. From afar they'd appeared like paintings, patterned with bands of concentric circles. Closer, Amber sees that the rings are lines of spinifex hummocks that trace the contours of each hill – spinifex growing through stone. She pulls over. It seems a good place for a break.

At a standstill, the whir of the engine slowly fades and quiet comes, an all-consuming quiet that is hard to find anywhere anymore. The drive still hums in her body, marks the sharp distinction between herself and the country around. She is full of the road, as if she has swallowed it. She leans against the Toyota, warm at her back. 'What a relief.' Her words tumble into the quiet.

Out here, maybe just for this moment, she feels unbound. Nothing to bind this country, or her, to time. This was the relief of it. The illusion of timelessness. Time uncatalogued by years and decades; days looping into nights into days, like an endless garment being knitted, with no design and no measure of completeness. To be outside time. Then she thinks of Andrew. The toll time has taken on him. What could happen in the two weeks she is away?

She wanders over to the foot of the hills, towards a cluster of giant spinifex. The insides of these doughnut-shaped tussocks are flattened beds of densely matted dead leaves and stems measuring about a metre across. Strange how the interior can die while the plant keeps growing, outwards and away. She steps inside one of the massive tussocks, careful to avoid the wall of sharp-tipped blades and stalks. The centre is like carpet, surprisingly benign. She crouches down, then lies on her side, drawing her knees to her chest. It is like a giant nest. She has seen kangaroos resting in these spinifex rings, like this, sheltered from the wind. The sense of peace is profound.

The Lord is my shepherd;
I shall not want.

He makes me down to lie
In pastures green; He leadeth me . . .

A psalm. A hymn they used to sing at church on Sunday, when she was a child. When the idea of God was comfort enough. Strange to still find solace in these lines. Stranger, perhaps, to think about green pastures out here. Her own pasture, she knows, is this red desert country, spotted with trees and shrubs. Both pasture and shepherd at once. 'The earth is my shepherd. I shall not want – for walls and fences.' She reaches to remember the rest of the psalm.

Though I walk in the shadow of death
Yet will I fear no ill . . .

The shadow of death. She shudders. She wrenches herself up, begins to dust her jeans. A trail of red sand spiders down the black denim. She decides to leave it. She goes back to the Toyota and climbs in. Through the dusty windscreen, a rippling band of blue mountains conceals the community where she will stop for fuel. If she takes a short break there, she can carry on to the next community, two hundred kilometres further on, where she can stay overnight and continue in the morning.

FOOTBALL AND FUNERALS

The main street is crawling with cars when Amber pulls in to get fuel. There are people everywhere. She stops at the store, where more cars queue for petrol. A mangy black and white dog is curled up under an abandoned stroller just outside the shop door, unbothered, it seems, by the streams of people spilling out, paper bags sweaty with greasy takeaway, cans of soft drinks clutched in their hands. Kids scuttle about, stripping the wrappings from sweets and throwing them to the wind.

Amid the chaos, she looks for traces of the community she first visited ten years ago. She'd stopped for fuel on the way to pick up some old people to take them to town for respite. The steel cage around the fuel pump. She'd never seen that before. Having to go into the shop to get someone to unlock it and fill them up. People singing country and western songs, which seamlessly spun into Christian hymns, into a microphone up the street. In the open air, in the heat. White government cars moored outside the council building like sailboats in a harbour. She recalls two or three young people drifting past, and though they'd kept a distance, she could see the cans pressed to their faces. It had taken her a few moments to realise what they were doing. Sniffing petrol. Their eyes watched her over the rims of the cans, vacant. She'd felt like an intruder, seeing things she shouldn't have seen simply because in such small communities there were few places to hide.

At the side of the shop a circle of men are gathered. One of them, somewhat taller than the others, leans against the wall like a ladder. Not old, not young, maybe in his sixties. He wears jeans and a red and black checked flannelette shirt rolled at the sleeves. A car pulls up and another man steps out and approaches the group. He offers his hand to each of the men in turn. One by one, the men bend forward to shake his hand, eyes to the ground. That beautiful gesture she'd forgotten. Not so much a handshake as the lightest touching of hands. Somebody has passed.

There are so many people still arriving, milling around the store. Amber realises it is about to close for lunch. While she fills the car, she looks around for a familiar face but it's only later, when she's about to drive off, that someone calls her name. A group of teenage girls approaches, led by Lisa. It is years since Amber has seen her but the young woman's manner is confident, as if she's been expecting her to turn up.

The girls clamber around the car, peering into the back. 'Any food?' a younger girl asks.

Amber laughs, charmed by the cheek.

'Hey!' Lisa growls at the girl like one would a puppy. 'Which way you headin'?' she asks Amber. She has no shame in turning the situation to her own advantage. 'You goin' to the football? Can we get a ride?'

The football. That explains all the people. Amber turns back to the loaded car and they laugh together at the absurdity of fitting all of the girls in, let alone driving a hundred metres to the other side of the oval.

But Lisa opens the passenger door and jumps in, followed by another tall girl who Amber doesn't know. Behind them, four or five girls push and squeeze into the back seat, determined to fit between the boxes and bags. They do not hesitate to throw Amber's things over the back to make room.

Amber winces to see her camera bag and tripod flying. 'Hey! Not the computer!' She stops them before the pelican case is turfed over the back seat.

'Sorry,' they say and hunch down low.

'So, you're here for the footy?' Lisa nods, half-distracted. Her eyes are on the stereo. She presses the eject button on the CD drive, which is empty. 'Any music?'

Amber laughs. 'Nothing.'

Lisa frowns.

Amber has so many memories of driving around these communities, young people crammed in the car, music blasting. And all these memories carry soundtracks. Akon, Shakira, 50 Cent. Then there was Lajamanu Teenage Band's 'Prisoner', which always felt to Amber like an anthem of time and place. 'Things are changing in the outside world today,' went the lyrics, which could well have been about the world beyond these lands. It made her sad to hear young people singing along, with such passion, 'I'm a prisoner, in this lonely world.' Cruising around communities, picking up young people, driving out to waterholes, grimacing at the thought of the CD getting cut up by the corrugations. It's like nothing has changed. But then it has. Everything has changed.

'When did you come?'

'Last night we come. Jennifer here ... Shyanna ... Brianna.'

'And Lena?'

Lisa's face looks grave at the mention of her grandmother. 'She been have a stroke.'

'No! When? I didn't hear. Is she in hospital?'

'She home now. She went in the aged care. But she home now.'

How out of touch she's become.

Lisa is distracted by cars turning up, people gathering at the oval, which is more of a basin of cocoa-like dust with white goal posts at either end. 'Other side.' She points to the side of the oval set against the hill. The bulk of red sandstone rock and the boulders below are striking against the muted midday sky. It isn't far, but arriving by car will give the girls the vantage point they need to survey the scene without committing their presence. The back seat is a cacophony of giggles and jabs as they check out who's here from neighbouring communities. They duck down. 'Go round, go round,' they boss her. Amber laughs.

She swings the car around the side of the oval and finds a spot where a few other families are parked near a small rocky outcrop. Her passengers are pleased with this position, out of the way enough to hide yet with a full view of the scene. Behind her, the backseat girls vie for a view in the rear-vision mirror, twisting and twirling the front strands of their hair, smoothing down their newly plucked eyebrows. The tall girl opens the window and leans out to fix her hair in the side mirror. Lisa swiftly reaches across to the door handle and pushes the door open, cascading into raucous laughter as the girl is propelled towards the dirt. She clutches the rim of the open window to catch her fall. The tall girl reaches back and slaps Lisa across the shoulder, who leaps out and chases her around the car.

The girls' squeals soon attract attention. 'Lisa!' They all look round. Across the oval, Lisa's sister Brianna is calling from a crowd of kids. She is much younger than Lisa, maybe eight or nine. Brianna makes a questioning gesture with her hand in the air, like a back-to-front L, and Lisa calls back, 'Amber!' When Brianna makes it across, she heads for the bush and starts snapping branches for kindling. She is followed by a group of smaller girls, about five or six years old, including her little sister Shyanna, forced to run around the perimeter of the oval as play recommences. The older girls retreat to the base of the hill, disassociating themselves, it seems, from their younger siblings.

Slowly, Amber recognises the confident strut of their mother, Jennifer, as she makes her way towards them with another woman. It's her sister, Mona. Every so often the women stop to talk with groups of people sitting in circles and clusters around the periphery of the oval. Amber looks at her watch. It's getting late. But there's no harm in staying for a bit. She has time. She planned for an overnight stop somewhere. If there's room at the visitors' centre, this may as well be it.

The little girls hover around the back of the car like bees at a flower when they see the carload of food Amber has brought with her. 'Can we make sandwich?' Amber inches the back doors open, careful not to knock anyone standing too close. They push and elbow each other out of the way. 'No, *me*.' 'What's your name again? You said me, eh? You said *me*?' It is one of those moments with kids where Amber wonders what remaining criteria you have to call upon to make a choice. The youngest. The eldest. The first one finished. The one who helped clean up? 'Brianna asked me first.' She settles it.

Brianna starts to pull out slices of white bread and arrange the pieces across the edge of the boot in neat rows. An age-old ritual, she renders it pure. Like a mother. The handkerchief hem of her skirt hangs around her ankles like she's playing dress-ups. Amber can only find a butter knife so the slices of ham are jagged and rough, but fortunately she has packed single squares of sliced cheese. Brianna carefully deals these out to each sandwich like playing cards. Little squares of plastic floating on the wind. Amber tries to catch what she can as they sail out the back of the car, then she sees the rubbish that surrounds them. Plastic bottles, baked bean cans and faded Redskin wrappers carpet the ground where people have come to watch the football. Up the hill, plastic bags are snagged on small trees. Broken glass glistens in the sun.

As Brianna builds a lofty stack of ham and cheese sandwiches, Amber keeps an eye on the industry. Not because Brianna isn't capable, but the scene seems somewhat fraught in the charge of an eight-year-old, now teetering on tiptoes to reach the spread. Two by two she stacks slices of filled-up bread to construct a precarious tower. Now a few camp dogs turn up and watch with hopeful eyes and wet mouths. It looks as though they are trying to be still so they won't be noticed and shooed away. The other kids kick a punctured football way too close. Every now and then it near-misses the sandwiches, and Amber calls out 'Wanti!' Brianna growls and the kids hold their hands over their mouths, calling in a sing-song chorus, 'Sor-ry!'

By the time Jennifer and Mona arrive, the girls have a small fire going. The women embrace Amber, 'maḻpa wiṟu', *good friend*. She pulls a canvas tarpaulin out of the car and lays it out for them to sit on. Jennifer inspects Brianna's fire. 'Kungka!' she calls to Amber. *Woman!* 'Kapaṯi?' Amber smiles to herself as she rummages through the back of the car for the billycan and cups. She'd forgotten how people bossed you around. But she is happy to make tea for the ladies. It makes her feel useful.

They spend most of the match drinking tea and talking. Amber is glad no one asks much about where she's been. People seem happy enough that you appear now and then. They fill her in with all the news. Babies, troubles, health. And death. A list of deaths, it becomes. *Sad news*, people say. *We have sad news.* You wince. Wait for the name, which can't be said aloud, but may be passed around on whispered breaths. When she was growing up, the priest would read out the names of the dead at church, so people could pray for their souls. Here the names of the dead are not spoken. Instead, people talk around them, identifying the deceased by community, by family, by character.

Jennifer tells her about the old man who has passed away. Amber remembers him. The funeral is tomorrow, back in her community. Of course. It is always like this. Football and funerals. The shadow of death always circling, sometimes swooping low.

'We used to get those rations, you know, from white people.'

Jennifer appears to have changed the subject.

'That's where it started, you know.'

'Uwa.' Her sister agrees.

'Flour, sugar, sweet tinned milk, tin o' meat.'

The two women reel off introduced foods like a litany learned by heart, sometimes in chorus, sometimes taking turns.

'A lot of our people on that machine now. From that sugar.'

'Uwa,' Amber agrees.

'Like that old man now,' Jennifer adds, and Amber sees how she's been talking in a roundabout way about the cause of the old man's death. He ended up on dialysis in town, almost blind.

'We had our bush foods,' Jennifer goes on.

'Healthy food,' says her sister.

'Healthy food,' they say together.

Amber thinks of the faded lolly papers strewn in the dirt. One time she was out driving with some older women. They might have been going for a picnic. They'd called out for her to stop when they spotted ngapari on the leaves of a stand of gums close by a creek. They'd scraped the sweet lerp from the leaves then sucked on them, delighted by the taste. But the young people had stayed in the car, and screwed up their noses when the ladies offered the ngapari to them. Sugar had spoiled their grandchildren, the ladies told her.

'We got no car,' Jennifer announces towards the end of the match, giving Amber, it seems, the information she needs to make the offer.

'How'd you get here?'

'We come with Joseph. But that car finish now . . . flat battery.' Jennifer tilts her head to one side.

Amber feels a small hesitation. Passengers are bound to slow her down. But it is the right direction. How to tell if the wind is at your back or blowing you off course? She is happy to see this family. 'I can take you home. I can drive that way.'

'Funeral tomorrow, for that old man,' Jennifer says. 'You might come.'

Amber feels a strange sensation in her belly. A swell of butterflies, disturbed.

'No,' she corrects Jennifer, too quickly, too emphatically. 'Not me. But I can take you home.'

She had known that old man. She met him in the community years ago and had seen him several times in town. He'd reminded her of a wizard with white whiskers and a crooked body bent over a cane. But she won't be going to the funeral. She doesn't have time. She hopes to reach her destination by tomorrow night.

All at once Jennifer is packing up, swilling warm water in the teacups to clean them and tossing it on the dirt. Then she lifts herself from the ground. Mona and Amber follow. 'We need to take one old lady,' she says, picking twigs and leaves from her nylon dress. Amber is unclear how many people are expecting a lift. Jennifer must see her calculating. 'She family for that old man,' she asserts. 'Must be room for her.'

The old lady is sitting on a wire bed frame at the side of the house when they pull up. She is bent over a canvas, one leg dangling at the side of the bed, painting. As soon as she hears the car she is up. She grabs a small cloth bag that is hooked over the corner of the bed frame, and starts to roll her blankets with a strong single arm.

Amber recognises her face. She is an artist. She'd seen her at the art centre when Amber was doing school holiday activities in her community. The story goes that this lady used to sit in the art centre with all the other ladies, for years. Then one day she'd picked up a paintbrush herself. And that was it. That was only ten years ago, when she was already in her mid-sixties. Now her paintings are sold all over the world. She has the same name as Amber's grandmother, now passed: Mavis.

Amber helps the old lady collect the tubes of paint hurled on the ground as she rips up the bedclothes like the roots of a plant. She bundles the bedding under her wing and takes the wet painting in the other hand, waving it gently in the dry air as she walks to the car.

The coming home car

Singing begins in the coming home car. Everyone pressed together. The ladies like bookends on the back seat, the two little ones in between. Bodies submerged in a swirl of faux mink blankets, patterned with tiger and zebra prints. Silhouetted in the fading light, the line of bodies might be a miniature landscape of rocky ranges, a series of peaks and saddles that belong to each other.

Lisa sits beside Amber, pressed against the passenger window. Her mouth is shut, eyes fixed ahead. Her teenage body closed, untelling. She didn't want to come. There was talk of her staying with her aunty in the community overnight and getting a lift back in the morning, but just as they were about to go, the conversation had turned to her. Her mother wanted her home. Jennifer had sent Brianna back to get her.

They'd waited in the car while the eight-year-old hobbled across the football field barefoot, stopping every now and then to pull a prickle from her foot. They all watched keenly while Brianna negotiated the deal with her older sister, who stood in a gang of girls in the middle of the dust bowl. All the time the little girl kept turning her head back to the car, towards the rumbling engine, as if checking her reinforcements were ready. While Lisa yelled and swore, Brianna stood, skinny legs pegged to the ground, bulletproof. But when their mother decided this had gone on long enough, she wound down the window and let out a shriek that parted the sea of young women. They ebbed away, exposing her elder daughter.

Lisa spat at the dust and marched behind her sister, all the way looking down. When she got to the car, she climbed up, lumped herself on the front seat, then slammed the car door. 'I'm hungry,' she snarled.

Now the youngest, Shyanna, is moulded into her mother's side, ready for sleep, Brianna beside her. But when Jennifer starts with a children's song, the little girls can't resist. The singing makes Amber happy. As a child, whenever her family travelled long journeys in the car Amber would sing. She'd spend hours transcribing lyrics from record sleeves and cassette covers, which she kept in a special cardboard folder in preparation for such journeys. The folder had once been a menu from a Gold Coast restaurant, given to her by her grandmother. It had flowers on the front. Pink hibiscus, green ferns, yellow-centred frangipani. Her mother often told the story of how Amber would refuse to sleep. Her head would drop, her neck would strain. 'Why don't you sleep?' her mother would say. And, wrenching herself out of any moment of failed composure, she would draw her back upright and brace her body against the pull of sleep, as the car crossed miles of country. Until the nodding would begin again. She wanted to be awake, as she does now. Awake and watching.

Jennifer encourages her daughters to sing in their language, old songs remembered from her own childhood. Her voice runs smooth as honey, keeping everyone in tune. When the song is finished, Brianna starts another. And so it goes for a while, with her little sister gasping and swallowing like a fish to keep up. Shyanna sings with a serious face, making them all laugh as she substitutes words with ones she's made up, mouthing in time no matter what comes out. Lisa tries to swallow her smile, lest anyone notice her happiness.

Circular songs go on and on, holding Amber in a happy memory of family. Until the songs run out, and the talking runs out, like they're ul̲tu, *empty*. And in the empty they open up, each of them, to their insides.

Long shadows. Sunlit hills. Soft rocks on the tired old road that pulls them on along the tracks of previous tyres. Like the grooves of a well-played record. They plough the powdery dust, swerve dishes of hardened mud. They track the road, erratic and pockmarked. Foreign objects flash in the fading sun, lie stark on a monochrome road. Plastic drink bottles, shredded tyres. Shafts of smashed tail-lights shimmer. Signs are made from freestanding car bonnets and ripped-off car doors, words sprayed on with paint.

Upturned cars, run off the road, rest like wounded beasts. Some burnt out, others stripped back, like roadkill pecked to bone. Sometimes the newly abandoned carry a clutch of branches on the bonnet – a sign that the owners will be back. But those abandoned are slowly transformed by the elements, soon camouflaged by the pinks and browns and deep red hues of the country, to become in time as much the landscape as the hills and trees. They tell of a country of car troubles and lives taken by these roads. But despite this, they still seem like beautiful objects, in the way of old and broken things. The way they glow like burnt toffee in the afternoon sun.

She has been in one of these vehicles, rolling, rolling. The mammoth Troop Carrier Amber was driving all at once reduced to a tin toy that tumbled off the edge of the road. Her body retains the memory of the vehicle starting to sway, then fishtailing violently from side to side across the span of the road. Of trying to right the steering wheel. Realising they were going to roll and there was nothing she could do about it. The tilt of the world and the slant of the sky. Holding on, holding on. Thump after thump after thump. Even when the vehicle had settled and all was static, she continued to try to right the wheel.

The silence that followed. The throbbing silence. Her friend in the passenger seat said later that the engine was making this awful whirring sound. Amber doesn't remember sound. She remembers hanging for a long time, unable to orientate herself. Watching drops of bright red blood spot the ground. When she finally worked out how to release the seatbelt, she fell hard onto her friend in the passenger seat. The car was on its side. The effort of heaving against gravity, trying to lift her leaden body from on top of her friend. The slowness of it all. Trying to think how to get out of the vehicle. (Later she would attribute this excruciating slowness to concussion.) Then crawling, increment by increment, up through the smashed window, careful not to cut herself, like an insect clawing its way out of its soon-to-be-discarded shell. She remembers the country, mute. Stretched out and still, profoundly still. Uninterrupted. The shock of this apparent indifference. The astonishment of brushing death, of being alive.

So now she sees fallen cars as stories too, and wonders what happened to each of them. A terminal breakdown? An accident? No recovery vehicle come to retrieve the wreck. Such events slip into the land, take their coordinates in a country that conceals its own substratum of stories, invisible to the untrained eye. They make a story of us too, of course, spinning across the topsoil, with no knowing when we might slip – no knowing when it will be our own time to be reclaimed. Amber shudders at the thought of it, the responsibility of the driver.

Soon the coming home car resounds with the heaving breaths of people sleeping. Orchestral collisions of breathing and snores, each with its own rhythm, somehow bring comfort.

Lisa leans into her, her face soft against Amber's shoulder, her body warm. It makes Amber feel good that she is so comfortable with her. It makes her feel part of the landscape of this family.

'Slow. Slow.' Even though she sleeps, Jennifer's voice stays in her head. 'Keep going, keep going. Ilaringanyi.' We're *getting closer*. She traces the night road with the high beam. The world is reduced to what is lit. Trees slice the grey, strips of inky silhouette. The smudge of distant hills.

She's not been this way before, as far as she can remember, but Jennifer assured her it was a short cut. She's always up for taking a road she's never travelled but didn't expect the navigator to fall asleep. She should be right if she stays on the main track.

'How far is it?' She'd tried to get some gauge from Jennifer about the distance home. 'Ila,' was Jennifer's response. *Close.* But proximity is skewed on such a scale, and the meanings of words thrown open. In the darkness, communities sit at unknown intervals. How far the journey between? Might be an hour, might be two. Might be more. If she refrains from measuring on the clock, it *feels* like a long way, as they dip through creeks and drift over dunes the road has claimed. 'Keep going, keep going. Ilaringanyi.'

Ilaringanyi. *Getting closer*. They'd played a game as the sun went down.

'Yaaltji Mina?' *Where is Mina?*
'Ilaringanyi.'
'Yaaltji Tjiwa?' *Where is Tjiwa?*
'Ilaringanyi.'
'Yaaltji Punu?' *Where is Punu?*
'Ilaringanyi.'

'Yaaltji Green Acres?' She'd thrown into the mix.

'Ai?'

Green Acres was the name of the cattle station where she grew up. From here, it seemed a million miles away – as far as childhood, and as much concealed.

THE CHILD OF THE HIGH SEAS

Darkness loosens the fixtures of linear time, and Amber drives on, the small container of the car her only anchor. Donkeys appear in the headlights. Silently they stumble into the unlit, disappear into the edges of the road. Like scenes from a dream being slowly remembered. Shyanna stirs on the back seat. Her eyes open, big and black, pools of glistening ink. It is as if she has been wrenched from the underworld and startled by the hard light of day. She stares, squints. 'Shy-anna?' Amber tries to comfort her with a sing-song tone. The little girl looks at her without words, then her eyes close like shutters and she is gone.

All along the road Amber has sensed the child behind her, her presence so visceral she might be carrying her on her back. Limbs dreaming out of the thin blanket, belly-up across her mother's knee, the limp child, the child as warm as breath. Her presence stirs something.

When Amber was about eight or nine her brother read her a story. It told of a child adrift in the middle of the ocean. She doesn't know how her brother came across this story. It had the sensibility of a children's story, with fantastic imagery and impossible happenings, but it can't have been written for children, as it became quite violent.

The daughter of a sailor, the child had died while her father was at sea. One night after her death, her father had thought of her for a long time, with such terrible intensity, that the force of his longing had conjured her to the surface of the ocean where she existed interminably, in a floating village. *Whenever a ship approached, even before it was perceptible on the horizon, the child was seized with a great sleepiness and the village disappeared completely beneath the waves.*

When no ships were in sight, the child spent her days wandering the watery streets. She went about her business, a series of daily rituals – opening the shutters of the red-brick houses, lighting kitchen fires, collecting fresh bread from the bakery. At night she closed the shutters and lit candles. Sometimes she sewed by lamplight. Time didn't pass in the floating village. The child was always twelve years old. Every day she walked to the village school. Sometimes she wrote down sentences, harnessing all of her concentration: *Night, day; day, night; clouds and flying fish . . . I thought I heard a noise. But it was only the noise of the sea.*

They'd been staying on the island when her brother read this story to Amber. So it must have been school holidays. It might have even been the first time her family stayed at the house on the island that would later become her brother's. They'd sat side by side upon a single bunk bed in the bedroom, backs pressed against the thin fibro wall that did little but muffle the reverberation of the television in the next room. It confounded her to discover, as an adult, that the story her brother read was not in fact illustrated. Translated from the French, it was written in the 1930s by surrealist writer Jules Supervielle. Somehow the distant murmur of the sea, the night, opaque outside the open window, the writer's words – all conjured for her an enduring image of a girl face-up on a ruffled sea that would be forever fixed.

Tonight, the story filters forward in time as if to find its place. It settles here, in the endless saddles of the road, so far from the sea. The night so black outside, it masks all landmarks and bearings, turns the solid world to liquid, the land to inky sea.

The child on the back seat might be her, being carried by the invisible current of the family car. Her mother singing as the night air knifes its way through the unsealed windows of the sea-green station wagon. The country gilded by headlights as they plough the corrugated road. Her brother beside her on the back seat, their legs overlapped under quilted cotton sleeping bags. Her brother's body is limp with sleep but she is awake and watching. If she tries, she can feel the print of the seams in the vinyl car seat pressing into her skin.

She can follow the line of her father's shoulders as it falls into the gap between him and her mother. Her mother's own outline is silhouetted by the rebound of the headlights on the road. Her shoulders are rounding. Her mother's and father's conversation rises and falls, belongs to its own landscape. Her mother plays her part like a child learning to play an instrument. Her offering is fragile, curled at the end. She waits for a response before she offers more. Her father's voice enters with a familiar certainty. He sets the pace, leads the movement of the duet that began before Amber could speak. A composition she can recall at will, at any moment of her life.

A long drive, out of one landscape, into another, that began by reciting the rosary. It was something her family always did on long drives. The disorientation of darkness and the solace of repeated prayer, grounded by the pod-like plastic beads running through her fingers. A memory that until now seems to have held no substance, only weight. Like a dream whose details you can't recall that nevertheless leaves you awash with feelings so strong you know something has transpired while you slept. The dream that disintegrates in the telling.

Not words. Never words are heard when she reaches back. More the timbre of each voice, the tension of the interplay between her parents, the mood of the composition. In front, the headlights reach forwards, dispelling the darkness temporarily; behind, the country falls to blackness.

She sifts through her body for remnant maps and memories that might recover her. Most of her early memories of road trips are of returning to the cattle station where they lived, coming back from day trips to neighbouring towns. All the time coming home. But for this one. It is the memory of leaving that country forever, and entering another. The memory of going to the city. The memory of leaving home.

When they travelled out of the country into the city, Amber was six years old. The first migration. Her father at the helm, his clipped black hair, sometimes turning slightly inward towards her mother. But mostly he looked straight ahead. *Turn around.* What is the age of his face back then? She cannot recall. Ahead there were doors that opened if you stood in front of them. Her brother told her. He'd gone with her father one time to visit their grandparents. He talked of tall buildings like they'd seen on TV. And girls and boys went to separate schools with many classrooms stacked one on top of the other.

She didn't want to be separated from her brother. The school they'd gone to in the country, her first school, had only sixteen children in total. So, although she was three years younger than her brother, when she started school they had shared the same classroom, the only classroom, the same teacher. Her brother beside her while their father drove them into what would be the next stage of their lives. Her brother's breathing, slow and steady and certain. It is possible that parents compose their children's lives to a certain age – or maybe forever have at least a hand in it. Somewhere stopped. A finished something. The kids wrapped in sleeping bags and blankets on the side of the road while their father changed a flat tyre. The world around them expanding like darkness.

They took the long road out of one country and into another. Into the city with sealed streets, uncreased and even. With too many people and too-tall buildings that blocked the sky. A house in a street and neighbours pressed close. The contours of the country bituminised, bricked and concreted over. The world overtipped and forever shaking. How to right it again? She'd stretched herself beyond sleep for as far as she could to chart the journey. After all, they were entering *terra incognita*. Here might be dragons. But as they sailed into dark and murky waters on that distant night – out, out, beyond the map – not even Amber could resist the call of sleep.

She jolts with the frightening thought that she may have been falling asleep. The weight of Lisa's body, slumped against hers, is pressing in, pinning Amber against the car door. Her left shoulder is starting to ache with the effort of keeping the girl from collapsing across her lap. Slowly the proximity becomes stifling. Amber flinches, tries to shift again, but the weight of the young woman follows her. She opens the window a little and sucks in the night air. She hears her own heart beating. *Slow down, slow down.* She just wants to get there now.

The floating village

Then from the silence, a thin voice in the dark. Amber checks the mirror. The old lady is pressing her forehead against the window, squinting into the blackness. She appears to be talking. Soon she starts to nod, as if affirming what she is saying to herself. Her body begins to rock gently, then effortlessly her speech trails into song. The high-pitched singing runs as far as her breath can carry her, falters while she gasps for air, begins again. Now sometimes speaking, sometimes singing, one form flows seamlessly into the other. For some time it goes like this, and Amber feels like a child come across something secret – something so beautiful, so rare, it beckons to be shared. But she is the only one awake. In a car, somewhere in the middle of the desert, in the middle of the country, a solo voice is singing stories. 'Shh . . .' It is like being inside the kernel of the secret itself.

Then silence again on the back seat. Outside the country mirrors the quiet, as if a light had skimmed across a certain stretch; now all is fallen dark. Or whatever was there has slipped irretrievably beneath the waves. The old woman's mouth drops open, cupped to the cold night air. Water sits in shallow wells in the grooves around her eyes. And Amber's also. *Night, day; day, night; clouds and flying fish. I thought I heard a noise. But it was only the noise of the sea.*

As well as being an artist, Mavis was a ngangkari, a traditional healer. Amber had been surprised to find this out. She's not sure what she expected, but somehow it didn't fit with what she first saw. When she met Mavis, she'd met a grandmother burdened with the task of looking after too many grandchildren. Her husband had passed away and all four of her children were in trouble of some kind or other. Mostly they lived in town.

Whenever Mavis came to the community centre, Amber would make the old lady a 'kapaṯi', while the children sucked on quartered oranges and played on the carpet with donated toys. But before long she started to hear of people going to Mavis for healing. Headaches, stomach pain, sadness. When she asked her about this work, the old lady had shrugged and smiled. But later she would tell Amber how in demand she was. How people came to her, often in the middle of the night, in all kinds of trouble.

People said she kept small stones and little pieces of wood in her handbag, or stashed somewhere in the house. Testament to the good work she'd done. Amber had not witnessed such an extraction, but since she'd lived in the desert she had heard many recounts of stones and fragments of wood being pulled from ailing bodies, to release the patient from their affliction. Sometimes she heard whitefellas speaking of the practice with an air of scepticism. The stones unsettled them. They belonged to the world of folk and fairytale, and couldn't withstand the scrutiny of Western science.

Amber wishes she could have had grief pulled from her body like this. That she could have shown it in an open palm, that people might have nodded and said they understood. She wishes she could have bottled it and buried it somewhere. Grief had clattered inside her like an undigested stone, for far longer than she wished. Until it no longer clattered but was simply a weight, as heavy and dense as wood.

'Tili! Tili!' Suddenly everyone is awake. Lisa withdraws her weight. 'Look! There's light!' The community is a peppering of distant but definite lights in a cleavage between the hills. It might be the floating village, street lamps alight, or a constellation of stars in a sky turned upside down.

Amber tries to imagine this sense of coming home, returning to the same location your whole life. She has had so many homes. She tries to imagine the sense of belonging that any one place might give. A rightful place. A place of return. A place to hold her as its own. Not that these communities are people's historical homes. The oldest of them is no more than about seventy years old, and was originally established as a mission and a buffer between the Aboriginal people and the encroaching settlers. It was a time when pastoral leases were swallowing traditional lands, and country was being increasingly cleared for grazing and herding, and waterholes were fouled by cattle.

But the country is home, the country is incontestable.

The sleeping child emerges and grips the back of Amber's seat. Shyanna whispers hot on Amber's neck, like an incantation, over and over, something. Lisa sees that she doesn't understand. 'She's gettin' happy,' she smiles.

In the quiet streets, dark figures cluster around front yard fires. Faces appear like downturned saucers of light. Heads turn slow towards the Toyota as it crawls alongside the houses. They go to the area where they have set up the sorry camp, a place for family until mourning is finished. Tents, tarps and mattresses make the makeshift camp, with fires dotted between, drawing people, draped in blankets, into closed circles. Amber helps the old lady down from the car, but before she has turned to say goodbye she is gone, dissolved into the darkness.

They cross the community and pull up alongside Jennifer's house. 'Nyangatja.' *This one.* It is not where Amber remembers the family living. But people move house all the time, sometimes because of death, sometimes for other reasons. Before she has even turned off the engine the doors fly open and her passengers start to spill from the car. Lisa peels away fully now, leaving a void in Amber's side. Cold rushes in.

The little girls slip by in silent procession, blankets dragging across the dirt. Seeing her mother lingering, Shyanna waits, her blanket shrouded around her head like a hood, her small hands clutching the folds close to her chin.

'Where you staying?' Jennifer asks.

'Visitors' centre,' Amber replies.

Shyanna lifts her chin, revealing a small, unhappy mouth. She looks at Amber accusingly. 'You said you was staying with us.'

Amber thinks what she might have said to cause this confusion. Perhaps she'd said she was *going home* with them, meaning to their community. Normally she would be pleased to have her own house, a comfortable bed. But she doesn't want to go to the visitors' centre tonight. She wants to stay with them. She looks to Jennifer. 'Is there room?'

Tonight it's cold and they will sleep inside, but Amber is pleased when Jennifer makes a fire out the back of the house. Lisa is cranky. She drifts inside and turns on the television. Jennifer ignores her. She puts a billy on and soon they settle themselves by the fire, the little girls curled beside their mother across a steel-framed bed, blankets drawn around them.

Later, Jennifer tells stories, her eyes electric with the drama, as they lie face-up to the night sky. Amber has missed these skies, crowded with stars. She has missed this country. She has missed these stories. She has missed laughter like this.

Jennifer's laughter lifts her like a swing. Tonight she will regale them all with mamu, *monster*, stories, and when the younger girls have gone inside she will start on her 'late night stories' – for women's ears only.

Lisa appears at the back door. She joins them around the fire. Encouraged by Amber's laughter, Jennifer embellishes her tales, adding bits here and there, like spices. Around them the community has gone quiet, apart from a solitary dog barking up the street, a TV in someone's yard. All the time Jennifer whispers low so that when they laugh, their laughter booms out, bursts the air, tight with silence. Trails of laughter linger like smoke.

One by one, houselights blink out. When they go inside and switch off their lights, there is the sense of all the houses, all the camps, all of them, being absorbed by the night. If a plane flew over, nobody would know they were here, disappeared in the darkness of the country. *But we are here*, Amber almost whispers aloud from her swag on the floor. *Listen*.

Beside her, the children's breathing loops the night air. Her own breath takes its part in the composition. In and out, in and out. Like they are threading themselves into the world. There is no knowing where any of them is headed, she thinks, what awaits them in their lives. When you're a child, you think life is endless, infinite. But there is no knowing at what point that thread might slip, when your breath will stop. And all that is before you is extinguished in an instant.

When she was Shyanna's age, she shared a bedroom with her brother. The first bedroom like a constellation she was born into. The arrangement of beds in that first house. Two single bunks with drawers below, a chest of drawers between them, laden with their things. A tin globe, most of it awash with pastel-blue sea. A stack of books with dinosaurs, monsters and dragons pressed between their pages. Precious stones, plastic jewellery, shells and feathers and fairy wands whittled from sticks and sprinkled with glitter, silver and blue and gold. A music box lined in pale blue satin, with a pink-skinned plastic ballerina who twirled on a tiny spring that bent over as you closed the lid. In here Amber kept holy cards, jewellery, a pair of prized rosary beads, with a tiny shaft of bone from one of the saints embedded in the back of a small timber cross.

She'd forgotten how she used to lie awake, watching geckos trail the tongue-and-groove ceiling. Listening to the high-pitched hum of mosquitoes outside the cotton net that shrouded her single bed. The ceiling fan that clicked with each rotation, like creaking bones. Breathing in the summer air, hot and soupy, before finally slipping into sleep.

FOR COMPANY

In the morning Amber draws herself out of the swag carefully. Everyone is still asleep, like a quiet landscape. Before the sun has reached the houses, she scrambles up the small stony hill behind Jennifer's place. The hill forms part of the rim of a rocky basin that contains the community. The wind has come today: she is halfway up before she realises the presence of the distant wailing. She catches her breath. So haunting, this high-pitched sound, drifting across the country from the sorry camp, so wild. Like a call to prayer ringing out from a minaret. This afternoon the funeral.

From the top of the hill she can see the way the settlement, once a mission, is laid out. Clusters of houses arranged by the compass: east side, west side, north side, south side. In the centre, a partly burnt-out church with reparations never finished, sides stripped back to steel skeleton. A band of brown-brick council buildings that from here look like cardboard boxes. An art centre with overgrown yellow grass all around, apart from some bald patches at the side, where artists sit and paint on the bare ground. And a shop, its entrance secured in heavy steel mesh painted canary yellow. To the north, the school and childcare centre, and another dusty oval. To the south, a stark strip of newly built townhouses: blue corrugated-iron boxes with front porches of freshly poured concrete and gleaming galvanised roofs. Beyond, hovering on the fringes of the settlement, the aged-care home. And behind it, obscured by the buildings, the sorry camp. Out of view, the sound of the wailing seems disembodied, ghostly. As if it is the country itself crying.

If it wished to, it would have good cause to cry. A sense of loss abounds here. The loss of land and languages and culture as people were forced to resettle on communities, or move to towns. The taking of children and the placing of many thousands of them in institutions. The nuclear tests that contaminated the ground and made people sick or blind. Alcohol, welfare, disease. So little time passed; so profound the interruption. Not all places carry the same story. Some had better policies than others. But she had forgotten the grief that is folded into the beauty.

All around are hills, solid and fixed. And beyond the hills, country sweeping outwards and away, a never-ending mosaic of sand and grasses, brushed blond by the morning sun. The real red sandhill country is further west, but even here the country retains the pink tint of rust. In some areas, dark marks score the pastel canvas, in patterns that repeat themselves over and over across the plains. They must be groves of mulga, growing in bands. Close up, their stick-like branches fan outwards towards the sky. Amber has sat under these trees many times when out with the women, digging for honey ants.

From up here, the country dwarfs the community in the middle of a nowhere that is somewhere to her now. For the more places she goes, the more she sees that there are no middles and there is no nowhere. But there are places of smaller scale, where the map might fold into a pocket – hand-drawn, if you like. Places you can clamber up the hills and let your spirit drift across outstretched land.

Soon voices drift up from below, the faint clatter of crockery, the TV. The house is awake. A dog sidles out the back door, sees her, begins to bark. Shyanna catapults out the door behind it, and clambers across the rocks and up towards Amber. She is wearing a pink long-sleeved T-shirt so big on her that it serves as a dress. The neck hole gapes over a bony shoulder. Underneath, she's wearing black tracksuit pants, but still she must be cold. The six-year-old skims, light-footed, across the surface of the rocks, barely checking her step. The scene is luminescent, with sunlight now streaming over the hill, casting the rock in a coppery glow. Shyanna's hair, rinsed scarlet-red, flares as she moves.

'What you doing?' the girl calls as she gets closer. She is smiling suspiciously, as if she's sprung Amber doing something she shouldn't have been. 'What you doing kutju?' *By yourself.* She pulls a sad face. 'Ngaltutjara.' *Poor thing.*

Amber laughs at the child's take on her solitude. 'I wanted to see the whole world,' she tells Shyanna, but the child takes a bird-like glance at the view, then yanks at Amber's arm.

'Let's go!' She pulls her up.

'Why did you come up all this way just to walk down again?' says Amber.

Shyanna is silent. Perhaps she doesn't understand. Perhaps she has been up here too many times to appreciate it. Perhaps she is cold. Then, when they are almost at the base of the hill, Shyanna replies, out of the blue, almost to herself. 'To get you – for company.'

Amber smiles, unsure what to say. 'Thank you!' she offers, but Shyanna bounces on ahead. She wishes she could be like her, unencumbered, free. Climbing the hill barefoot with her brother. Riding her bike, no hands, in the wind. Balancing along the timber fence rails in the stockyard with no fear of falling. Swimming out into the open sea.

Amber has floated in the watery solitudes, neither dead nor alive, for the past year. She has gone about her business each day – a series of rituals – which, if rendered perfectly, she has hoped might restore order, return balance to things. At night, she has closed the windows and prayed that sleep might move her forward, away from grief, before the earth revolves and night turns into day again. *Night, day; day, night; clouds and flying fish.*

This afternoon the funeral

The wind sketches lines and patterned scrawls across the country. Wind currents, mapped like tracks into this place, converge at this one day. Conversation carries on the wind passing, cars passing, people passing – to the shop, away from the shop, to the shop. Kids looping turnstiles. This afternoon the funeral.

In this country, time is dealt out differently. A day is not divided into thirds by breakfast, lunch and dinner. Here, a day seems to unfold one limb at a time, and stumble forward towards its interruptions. You can sit around forever waiting for something to happen. Then someone says, 'Palya,' and everything shifts. It's time.

Stillness swells until it erupts into something. An engine revs, someone screams up the street, a dogfight snaps the stasis. And you are taken with it, like a willy-willy on a windless day. Caught up, carried to the end of it, until the wind drops and the day settles back into itself like a sleeping dog.

This is how it seems to Amber, ignorant of the pressures that gave rise to the eruption, outside of language. She doesn't mind, usually, to be pulled off track for a bit. There is always something to be gleaned, if you let yourself be taken by the back roads. But today she is conscious of being carried off course. And she is waiting for the wind to drop.

She expected to be gone by now. But when she returned from the hill this morning, Shyanna asked if she would make a cake with her. 'Like last time.' That must have been two years ago, when she was only four. Amber couldn't refuse. But they had to wait for the shop to open to get the ingredients.

They are back at the house when some ladies come to the door. Words are flung backwards and forwards across the room. Heads are shaking. Tongues clicking. When the ladies leave, Jennifer collapses on the couch. Her body slumps like a sigh. There are not enough pallbearers. Not enough legs for the coffin. That old man is lying flat in a box and there are not enough men to carry him. Last night there was drinking, she says. Fighting up the road. Today the youngfellas are hungover. The old ladies are pissed off. Who's going to carry the coffin?

Jennifer pulls herself up and goes to the back door. Outside, it's warmed up, though Jennifer has kept a low fire burning. The wind makes the fire spark, the flames leap. When the cake is cooked, Amber and Shyanna decorate it with sliced apple, making scalloped patterns with the curved wedges. 'Like nana's painting.'

Jennifer announces she wants to go to her parents' place, to see if her father is still coming to the funeral. Her mother is back home now, though she's been several weeks at the aged-care home recovering from the stroke. She tells Amber she should come.

Amber hesitates. She is happy to give Jennifer a ride, and she'd love to see Lena. But she is unsettled, as if she's hurtling towards something she cannot stop. She is still some way from her destination, which she had hoped to reach today. But it is early still. She can leave before the funeral. She goes with Jennifer.

Lena lives with her husband on the border of the street grid, so that from the back of the house you can see straight out to the ranges, out to her country. Lena and Alfie had grafted their 'camp' onto the side of Lena's sister's house when they'd moved in from their homeland. After Alfie hurt his leg and could no longer drive. It was difficult for them, leaving their ngura, their *country*, despite how challenging living out there often seemed. They were forever calling Jennifer, in need of help: the car had broken down, the cable for the television wasn't working, the power was out again.

It was just a little shack in a small valley between two hills, about thirty kilometres outside the community. It had a bore and a water tank. The shack was used only when needed. Mostly they camped outside, swags rolled out on iron bed frames to avoid snakes. They cooked on a fire and used a tap on the side of the tank for washing dishes. This was where they were living when Amber met them. When she first went there, she saw them as being without, but soon she came to see that, for them, the structures were ephemeral – things came and went, broke down, were buried in the dust. Their country surrounded them.

Whenever Lena came in to the community she'd visit the community centre, so when Amber was there, often on school holidays, she saw her. There'd always be a tangle of dogs at Lena's ankles. She'd walk around the back and sit under the shade of the awning, puppies swarming around her. Amber would bring her a cup of tea in an oversized pannikin. Two teabags, topped up with cold water to cool it down, and a generous splash of milk. 'Two full sugars.' Lena was Amber's language teacher, her cultural consultant, her guide in all matters.

Now the old couple's home is a patchwork of shelters cobbled together from random bits of salvaged steel, shade cloth and canvas. Since she was here last, the camp seems to have grown, with star pickets and ropes drawing extra canvas out from the main tarpaulin, rusted sheets of corrugated iron tacked together to make more wiltja, more *windbreaks*. They'd tried to convince Lena to stay at the aged-care home but she had refused. She wanted to be where people came and went, surrounded by her family, her dogs, her familiars.

Lena is stretched across a canvas swag, waist-deep in a mound of tan and black synthetic mink blankets, or 'minkies', as people call them. New puppies are tucked at her side. In the dim light the lines on her face appear like bark. *Timelines*, Amber thinks. Big eyes protruding from under a pink and brown beanie pulled firmly over her wrinkled brow. After this the old lady is a cacophony of colours and prints, with a green and black checkered flannelette jacket pulled over a powder blue, pink and red floral dress; then the black and tan stripes of the blankets. She stretches her neck to see who's come, but her head is heavy and she lowers it back to the pillow and rests at an awkward angle. Jennifer reaches to adjust her mother's head and the old lady clutches her hand. Shyanna climbs onto the swag, disturbing the puppies. She draws them close, lets them lick her face and giggles. She nestles into the side of her grandmother.

Amber drags a partially melted plastic milk crate over to sit closer. Jennifer asks her mother if she remembers 'the whitefella'. The old lady looks directly at Amber and smiles. 'Uwa.' She starts to speak. Her tongue is swollen so that it takes up too much of her mouth, gets in the way of her words. She is talking Pitjantjatjara. On and on. Amber understands some. Enough to listen harder. She knows Lena is talking about her homeland, asking her daughter questions. But mostly Amber finds herself listening to sound rather than content, nodding every now and then, 'Uwa. Uwa.' The lullaby of a foreign language.

The last time Amber saw Lena, they'd gone out hunting near her homeland. Her and her sister, two white-haired old ladies, legs straddled either side of a deepening hole, had sent the red dirt flying with sawn-off shovels. Then, like women half their age, they'd scooped out the soil with their strong arms, reaching into the holes. They'd hunted like this since they were girls, they told her. When the hole was deemed deep enough, Lena had lowered herself down, lain on her side and begun poking a thin stick into the darkness. Then, drawing it up, she'd run her fingers along the rough end, like she was checking the oil level in a car. 'Wiya. Nothing. Can't find 'im.' She was looking for hair – rabbit hair. On and on it went like this, hole after hole. Digging, digging, then the stick back down again. Six holes and no rabbits later, they'd moved on.

The ladies decided instead that day to gather mingkuḻpa, *bush tobacco*, which covered the country at the time. They ended up picking all morning, laying the green plants out in the tray of the ute like sleeping bodies so that Lena could take the harvest back to her homeland, where she would dry it out properly. That must have been three years ago. But Jennifer had told Amber yesterday, at the football, that her mother had continued to hunt, to harvest mingkuḻpa, on her ngura – despite being about eighty years old – right up until the stroke.

Outside, the wind has picked up and the canvas tarps are flapping. Inside, the air is trapped. A plastic fan, powered from the house, only spins the stagnant air at high speed. Inside is quiet, a quiet that is hard to come by. Not soundless. There is Lena's and Jennifer's talking, the whirr of the fan, the incessant buzz of flies. The rhythmic lap of puppies' tongues in an old tin flour drum that rests beside a gas cooker on the ground. Quiet is so often violated by traffic, television, telephones. Conversation so often interrupted by messages from someone else, somewhere else. Here, everything is simmered down to this small domestic dome.

She thinks of Andrew, back in town, in the stripped-back world of his bedroom. But when she does, it is not his face she sees. It is the face of her brother. She flinches, tries to unsee it.

In those days confined to his bed, her brother had kept on checking with his wife as to whether she'd remembered to close the side gate, to keep out the local dogs that would disturb the ecosystem he'd created for birds and other native wildlife. Since he returned to the island, he'd managed to restore the backyard from a bald patch of lawn to a layered landscape of trees and shrubs, native grasses and ground covers. He'd set up nest boxes and regularly recorded their usage, from breeding successes to predation. He wanted to know of any sightings by anyone staying at the house, and insisted they be recorded in a little green notebook that he hung by the back door.

Amber tried her best to comply, but was often uncertain of the distinction between species – currawongs and crows, rainbow lorikeets and scaly-breasted lorikeets, all the different kinds of honeyeaters. 'That's a rainbow bee-eater,' he would declare, when she reported her vague descriptions. Or: 'It sounds like a dollar-bird! It might be – they have been sighted here. You say the flight feathers and tail were definitely blue?' So she would become his eyes, when he could no longer leave the bedroom. It was the least she could do for him. Even from his bed, when he would hear them, he would become still, dropping words or concentration, and sometimes cock his head to listen more keenly, animal-like.

The old lady closes her eyes. Her eyelids are plump, swollen, the skin so dark it appears bruised. Her mouth falls open after a while. Like her brother, each time he slipped back to sleep. Amber recoils. She looks to Jennifer for permission to go.

Jennifer stands, gestures with her chin to Shyanna, who starts to unburden herself of puppies. Just then Jennifer's father appears in the doorway. The old man brushes past, lifts his head to acknowledge the young white woman and shuffles towards the gas cooker. Alfie seems frailer than Amber remembers, and his bad leg looks no better. He walks with a cane. At the doorway, Jennifer stops and asks him about the funeral.

'Palya,' he answers and she goes outside. Alfie draws a cigarette lighter from his trouser pocket and lights the gas, then bends to rest a billycan on the blue flame. 'Any tjuka?' He rifles through the torn sugar sachets scattered on the ground. Amber shrugs. He mimics her. 'Wampa,' they say together. *Who knows?*

They both laugh and Shyanna giggles shyly. Alfie squats to sit on the edge of his wife's swag and the little girl wriggles along. 'Ngaḻtutjara,' he shakes his head. *Poor thing.*

'Ngaḻtutjara,' Amber commiserates.

They are silent for a bit and Amber wonders what she should do. Jennifer might be waiting.

'Where you been?' the old man asks suddenly.

'Brisbane,' she says. It's a kind of summary for floating-in-the-watery-solitudes.

'Brisbane,' he repeats, as if it was a word only, unfixed to any meaning, and for a moment it sits there, an empty sound, clanging in the still air.

'In the city,' Amber offers.

'City too big,' he laughs out loud, revealing a mouth of missing teeth.

He is right. From here the city does seem too big. 'Big', from here, is bigger than before. Amber looks around. Blankets strewn and puppies stretched by the side of a sleeping lady, their black and tan bodies camouflaged by the colour of the rugs. The world in her is too big. She has cities stuffed into too small a body. Places only dreams recall. She has family and friends dispersed across the country, and she has stretched herself to behold them all.

From out the front comes a high-pitched yelp, and the puppies fly out the door, squealing. The old man springs to his feet, grabs his stick and staggers quickly onto the street. Amber follows with Shyanna. A pack of camp dogs are pulling each other apart. Ripping into each other. Locked together, they make a grotesque beast of limbs and heads and snarling jaws. Saliva whips all over the place.

The old man is light, like a stick that might be swept away by a small wind. He starts to beat at the many-dog-beast with his walking cane, his action compounding the awful yelps that won't cease. He belts into the beast until a few dogs are shed. They scurry away with turned-under tails. He thrashes the stick across the last of them until, finally loosened, they release their locked jaws and cower across to the other side of the street.

Alfie bends to gather up two of the puppies that have strayed onto the road. Shyanna helps her grandfather tuck them under his arm, then the old man begins to hobble back towards the house. Amber goes to say goodbye, but already he has his back to her. For a moment she is not even sure that he remembers she's here. 'Palya,' she says, announcing her presence as much as her departure.

He turns to her. 'You be see my daughter,' he says, 'kutjupa, *that other one* . . . You tell her . . . send blankets . . . for her mother.'

'Uwa,' she promises.

Amber had sometimes seen his other daughter in town. Jennifer's younger sister. Just before she'd left Amber was driving along one of the main roads, where the footpath serves as a well-worn track to the pub. A woman stumbled onto the road. Amber braked quickly, though she was well to the side of the vehicle. From the footpath, a man growled at the woman and limped out to drag her back. Amber recognised her. She offered to drive her home. On the way back to the town camp, the woman kept repeating, over and over, 'I was telling him, I know her, I *know* her.' But that was years ago.

What is the distance between town and this place? You can measure it by the odometer. But what is the distance to the old man? How far away is his daughter, and all the ones who have gone? How come she won't come back? How many messages get lost between these worlds? Even if Amber finds her, will his daughter send blankets?

She thinks of Andrew, lying in that bed, the things that might be bothering him, the things he can no longer attend to. And now she thinks of her brother. Blankets for the old lady, birds for her brother. These last requests seem worthy of fulfilling. She must help Andrew, though she doesn't know how. But she will make sure he has what he wants in the end.

Now that the street dogs have disappeared, calm returns. Jennifer is waiting in the car. The old man stops before vanishing around the side of the house. 'You can pick me up?' he calls. 'For that funeral.'

'Uwa,' says Amber, though she is unsure. Perhaps Jennifer is relying on her for the car. Yes, she can pick him up. Drop him at the funeral. But she won't be going. She will prepare food for afterwards. Do something useful. Then get out of here.

To the funeral

The old man is waiting on the street when they come back to collect him. He leans on his cane, his torso bent away from his legs as if his body is hinged halfway down. He is all dressed up, in a buttoned white shirt, black trousers hitched and gathered by a leather belt around his slight frame. He calls out that Lena wants to come. His daughter huffs, 'Ai!' She yanks the car door open and climbs out, leaving it gaping. Amber watches father and daughter argue on the street in language too fast for her to follow. Then the old man hobbles right past his daughter and climbs into the back seat, next to Lisa. He stares straight ahead.

Jennifer calls to Amber. They go inside to find the old lady swung over the side of the swag, propped up with pillows. A bundle of black and white clothes lie beside her. Lena looks markedly better than she did this morning but Jennifer is not happy. She is worried for her mother. Still, without saying a word, she helps the old lady into the funeral clothes. First, she widens the elastic waistband of the black skirt and threads Lena's legs through, one by one. Then Amber helps to lift her weight while Jennifer hoists the skirt up over her mother's hips. They ease the old lady into the wheelchair, then guide her arms through the sleeves of a somewhat crumpled shirt. As her daughter goes to fasten the buttons, Lena lifts her hand, and for a moment Amber thinks she is about to push Jennifer's hand away and do the job herself. But she doesn't.

For a fleeting second, she clasps her daughter's hand, squeezes it tight, then releases it, letting Jennifer finish the task.

On the way to the funeral they pass two children, who beckon them to slow down. As she pulls up, Amber recognises Brianna's face under her hoody. 'Any room?' she says. Amber laughs. Jennifer is in the front beside her, Alfie and Lena and Lisa squashed into the back seat, Shyanna on Lisa's knee. They are full. But Jennifer opens the car door and the girls scramble into the back seat, climbing across Lena and Lisa. There's always room.

They pull up near the churchyard, where a stage is set up with a PA system and a microphone. A bunch of children scuttle about, picking up plastic flowers from the dirt and returning them in clutches to the plastic vases that had been toppled off the stage by the wind. Some old people wait on white plastic chairs but mostly people are still arriving, tracking a path from the church to the shop, back to the church again. Camp dogs thread in and out of people's legs. Babies cry and children clamber for their parents' attention. Jennifer and Amber go around the back of the car to get the wheelchair for Lena. They lever Jennifer's mother down from the car and park her beside her husband in the sun.

Amber is about to leave when she senses, on the edge of hearing, the faintest drone. Almost inaudible. The Cessna engine coming in, of course. Bringing the body home. As soon as she is certain of its presence, it seems that silence falls across the congregation like a shadow eclipsing the sun. Then, just as soon, the wailing starts. One by one, women's voices join in on top of this first note until it is drowned in a shrill chorus of keening.

Wind brushes her face, too close. She feels a sense of spinning inside, and the spinning is gaining speed. As it swells, the wailing pierces her skin, prises her open, bores into her and doesn't stop. She cannot leave now.

They are using the ambulance in place of a hearse. As it approaches, the priest looks around. Who's going to carry the coffin? Restlessness prickles across the congregation. Lena has wet eyes when Amber turns to her. Alfie is agitated. He taps his cane against the steel frame of his wife's wheelchair. Amber catches his gaze by accident. The old man looks down. Amber feels ashamed. He is too frail to help. She wants to scream at those youngfellas to get down here and carry the fucking coffin.

Jennifer turns to a whitefella, a teacher from the school, who looks across to the motley group of men now gathered around the coffin. A ripple of nods passes through the group. The whitefella goes like it's an inevitability. He's not even family.

The coffin is carried across the dusty yard by a scraping of old and broken men. One whitefella at the rear. It's like watching the feeble limbs of an insect being crushed by its own weight. A praying mantis carrying the corpse of itself. The stillness of it. The ceremony of it. The swaying of the pallbearers backward and forward, backward and forward, in the cold wind. Like a house on stilts being blown about. A lopsided, jacked-up wooden box.

People come forward to lay flowers, all the while the wailing. Some linger, some collapse over the coffin, in heart-wrenching portraits of grief.

The high language of the service annoys Amber, so formal and lofty that it becomes almost benign. And why, she wonders, is such an important ceremony being conducted in English? She tries to let it wash over her but the frustration keeps returning with each neat offering by the priest, meant to comfort. She doesn't understand how Jesus dying gave us eternal life. Did she ever? *What does eternal life even look like?*

Then the priest passes the microphone around, and one by one people speak about the old man. The priest reads faxes from family who could not come. *Why do we only have good words to say once somebody's gone,* Amber thinks, *when it's too late?* Is this what funerals are for? To forgive ourselves the judgements, the jealousies, the failures we commit against our fellow humans every day? Not even enough limbs for the coffin.

The old man's public biography is recounted by the priest and reinforced by a number of speakers and letters that are read aloud. It is a big story. He grew up in the bush, then came to work at the mission as a young man. Worked on cattle stations. Had to learn a new language, an entirely new way of life. Ended up in town, on a dialysis machine, like so many. People add their memories and stories, and a sense of the old man soon fills the air. Amber thinks how our lives tell a twofold story. There is the story of an individual life, and there is the story a single life reveals about a particular place and time. This old man's story is also the history of Aboriginal stockmen in the 1960s, the story of the missions, of the changes in work, of equal wages. These stories settle with the congregation for a time, and will disperse when they go their separate ways.

They all stand as the pallbearers carry the coffin to the side of the churchyard, where the ambulance is waiting. As they pass, a woman near Amber throws herself to the ground, letting out a gut-wrenching wail. She might be his daughter? Amber joins others in the rush to help, but as they haul her up the woman lunges forward again, screaming and weeping at once. Two women lift her a second time, draping her heavy arms around the frames of their shoulders like outstretched wings. Amber finds herself jacked up under one of the woman's arms, her body continuously propelling forward, so that they have to push against the force of her to prevent her from falling.

Amber's throat is throbbing. She swallows. Again and again the woman collapses forward, until Amber thinks she cannot bear it, this woman who cannot hold herself up. Tears well inside her but will not break. Until she can barely breathe. Christian hymns blare out from the speakers, hymns she recognises, translated into Pitjantjatjara. Around her, people begin to sing.

Walkunila pitalytji pulka irnyantja
Mama wankaru Ilkaritja pukultjutu
Mayatjanya Milmilnga, Jesunya Christanya.

Lena is too tired to go to the cemetery. She wants to go home. 'Palya?'

Jennifer wheels her to the Toyota, and she and Amber help the old lady in. Lena grabs the handle above the open door and hoists herself up. Strong arms still. Jennifer folds the chair, and she and Amber lift and jam it into the back of the car. It's so heavy it takes every ounce of Amber's strength. Then, with so much other stuff in there, they can't get the door closed. Amber bashes it a few times until finally it jams shut.

Back at Jennifer's house, some ladies are settled by the fire as if weighted by the afternoon sun. But Amber is not settled. She is rattled by the funeral. She cannot believe she has lost another day, and Jennifer is still not back with the car. Campfire smoke coils quietly across the yard, stinging the corners of her eyes. She slips silently around the side of the house. Shyanna follows. She seems surprised by Amber's tears, or shy of them. She avoids eye contact. 'We're making a garden, look!'

Amber wipes the wetness from her face with her shirt sleeve. Moving in front of her, the little girl shows Amber the fence her family have erected, with green shade cloth stretched between star pickets. Around the inside of the square enclosure, she and her sisters have jabbed pink and orange plastic flowers into little stumps painted yellow. Then, pointing to a patch of dead grass in the corner, Shyanna says: 'Nana wanted to put grass there. She just put it there in the dirt. I tell her, "That's not how to grow grass!" It's all dead now, look. That's not how to grow grass, eh?'

Amber remembers Alfie, who might be back at the church by now. He didn't want to come with them, but said he'd go back to the churchyard after the cemetery. She'd offered to come back for him. She suggests to Shyanna that they walk up and check on him. Take him something to eat.

'We should take that cake, eh?' Shyanna says, excited.

They walk back to the churchyard, the little girl chatting all the way. Like a little motor, she keeps Amber above water, propelling her forward.

It's only a few hundred metres if they take the dirt track that cuts through the back of the houses. Amber carries a ham sandwich in a plastic bag for the old man. A cup of tea in a blue enamel pannikin. The wind blows dust in their eyes and Amber cups her hand around the hot drink. Shyanna has wrapped a generous piece of cake in a paper towel and carries it, warm in her hand. Camp dogs follow; they can't help themselves.

Amber used to take 'smoko' to her father up the track to the windmill on the cattle station. A thermos of tea. Her mother's cakes. Windmill turning slow against the still sky. She must have been about the same age as Shyanna. One or two years younger, maybe, walking at the side of her mother. Her brother would have been at school. Maybe they did this every day. Took morning tea to him wherever he was working. She doesn't remember. Only this one salvaged memory of the ritual. Up the track to the windmill.

When they get to the church there is no one there but Alfie and one young man, who is rifling through Alfie's bag like a dog at a rubbish tip. A camp dog. Hungry dog. Mad dog with mad eyes. Amber calls out, 'Hey!'

But the old man seems unperturbed as the young man slinks off, a few crumpled notes in his hand. 'Let him have it.' Alfie brushes a hand through the air. 'That's my grandson.'

Grandparents give to their family. Everybody gives to everyone.

'Mad one,' whispers Shyanna as she watches the young man scurry away. She makes a circling movement with her finger beside her head. 'Rama-rama.' *Crazy.* Alfie laughs with his granddaughter.

THE RIGHTFUL PLACE OF GRIEF

By the time Jennifer gets back, it's too late to get going. That night Amber stays at the visitor's centre. There are too many people at Jennifer's house, and she needs to be alone. The strip of blue corrugated buildings hovers like a satellite on the outskirts of the community. There are tradesmen staying next door. Their truck is parked in the drive. But the front yards are empty. No fires here. Inside, the potent smell of paint, the unscuffed tiles. The benches are clean, uncluttered. Everything is white – white walls, white ceilings, white cupboards and benchtops – apart from the pale grey floor tiles. Aluminium security doors screen the outside, slam behind her each time she brings in things from the car. Inside, she cannot feel the wind, will not hear the sunset wailing.

She lies awake, her body charged, electric. Over and over she feels the woman falling through her. The weight of her, the force of her. Like a wave crashing, a tree lopped, unstoppable. As if the current of death were so strong it had uprooted her also. Amber knows death to be this powerful, loss to be this violent. This is what it is to belong to another. To remain composed in the face of this now seems absurd.

She hadn't gone back for her brother's funeral. She couldn't explain this to anyone. No one said anything either way. Maybe she wishes they had. She didn't go back for her brother's funeral because she couldn't get on the plane. She had only been back a day and a night before the news came. Two flights it would have taken, with a stopover in between. She couldn't make the arrangements. She couldn't pack her clothes. She couldn't be in public.

She had only been to a handful of funerals in her life. She hadn't been allowed to go to her grandfather's, the first of her grandparents to pass away. And her grandmother's after that. She was twelve at the time. Had her parents hoped to spare their youngest child from grief, or had they not wanted their children to see their own?

The year after they moved to the city, her father read an article from the newspaper of a girl who was killed in a car accident. The girl was a friend of Amber's from the little country school she'd attended. She was older than Amber by three years, in the same year as her brother. But there were no girls in Amber's class of three, nor in the year above. Everyone shared the same classroom. Everyone played together. Age didn't matter. Her friend had pushed her high on the swing in the schoolyard at lunchtime. On Amber's sixth birthday, her friend had given Amber a toy dog, chocolate-brown felt, hand-sewn by her mother. Amber could see the present her friend had brought for her tucked under her desk all day.

There are parents who can read the finest fractures in their children's faces, can see shadows before the child has felt them fall. Amber believes this absolutely of her mother. But when she looks back at the day she heard about her friend's death, she sees that compounding the shock of the news was the scant attention given to it by her parents. She looked to them for signs of grief, perhaps for how to grieve.

Why hadn't they gone to the funeral? A child killed in a car accident. A child they loved, she thought. A child who could have only been ten years old. The same age as her brother. At the time, Amber imagined the world where they'd lived on the cattle station to be so far away, but last year she went back with her mother for the first time and was surprised to realise it was only a five-hour drive. Living out here, she saw how Aboriginal people crossed miles of country to attend funerals, all the time. Helping each other out with fuel, a place to stay. Taking time out. She remembers her father reading from the paper, but nothing more. No one said anything further about it. She had decided no one knew what gripped her heart – and she'd decided something else: grief was something you kept to yourself.

She asked her mother about this last year, when they went back. They'd gone to the town cemetery on the last morning and had come across her friend's grave. Her mother was surprised by Amber's tears, and struggled to remember the day the news had come. She said she may have been trying to protect her children, to 'play down the death'. But could death be played down? Could grief be bridled? *Played down*, grief grew like a monster, writhing, lurching inside, as if tangled in some kind of net. Can we be spared sadness, or does sadness, if unable to flow, only silt up?

The few funerals she had gone to were those of the grandparents or parents of school friends. She remembers pews of people choking on tears. Lamentation throttled by cloth and tissue. The sound of grief being swallowed was like a chorus of catching breath. As if sadness pressed outwards from people's insides, until their bodies were so tight the only way to breathe was to gasp at the church air.

Today the crying rang out across the churchyard, unbridled, unselfconscious. All throughout the service it ebbed and flowed; when all seemed finished, a single cry carried the sorrow of everyone. At the end of the service the communal crying flared again, a many-voiced beast, as if in the final throes of its life.

It wasn't so long ago, she thought, that our own forebears gathered in grief to wail their dead. In Ireland and Scotland, at least, the practice of keening was still happening up to the middle of the last century. *Keen*, some say, comes from the Irish *caoin*, for crying. Others maintain the original word is *cine*, which makes it almost identical to the Hebrew word *cina*, which tells of lamentation with the clapping of hands. There are people alive who remember the Irish practice still. Her grandmother once spoke of it. Official keeners, or singing mourners, led the lament. They were women, midwives of a kind, tasked with taking things from people's minds to their bodies. They were paid to do it, often with no more than a glass of whiskey.

There were official times to cry, just like here. Over the body, when the corpse left the house, at the gravesite. Sometimes the keeners would walk through the hills, followed by the grieving – rocking, kneeling, clapping – to let their loved ones know they were missed. They cried to the skies, 'Why did he die? Why?' When they passed by houses or villages, the wail would swell still louder, giving notice that the funeral was passing. People flocked and followed, joining the wild chorus, which was sometimes accompanied by the tearing of hair, the beating of breasts, the throwing of hands to the sky.

Once dirges accompanied by music, these death songs became in time more like mournful cries, destitute of words. *Uncomfortable*, they have been called. *Unearthly*. And, in time, unwanted by the church. The practice was discordant with their own ceremony, where the priest recited hushed prayers over the body, laid out for the wake. Perhaps it was at odds with the belief in the afterlife, to let death unsettle people so. Better to be glad that the dead had moved on to the next life, lifted from this valley of tears.

The Irish keeners would soon become like museum relics, spectacles for travellers who wished to see an Irish funeral. Soon the people themselves started seeing the practice as primitive, 'unearthly', and became ashamed. They felt they were being regarded as backward. And so, in time, they discarded it.

Was this keening unearthly, or is it we who have become unearthly, shunning the very things that make us human? Do we fear our grief will topple us and threaten our composure? That if we stop the clocks, we may not be able to start them again?

She has stumbled through the hills and parched rivers of this country, trying to rid herself of grief. 'Why did he die?' Amber whispered to the sky. 'Why?' She has rocked on the stony floor of her flat, cried out in guttural sounds she didn't recognise as her own. But this was behind closed doors. She has done it alone, without ceremony, and without comfort.

The week her brother died, the skies opened over the desert. Every afternoon, for days on end, the afternoons grew dark, compressed. Thunder rumbled. Heavy sobs of rain battered against the tin roof, thrashed the country, drowned out her crying. Rain that revived the rivers, that spilt and splayed across roads in torrents, sending traffic on various detours and stopping cars. Unable to pass by, passengers would often get out to stand and watch, mesmerised, as the mass of whirling brown water surged through the town, scooping up all in its wake, unbound and bold, as if reclaiming its rightful place in this country.

Every day after his death, Amber drove out of town, out west to a gap in the ranges. It was rare to see the creek flow through this particular place, but in that week, cocoa-coloured water gushed through the gap at considerable speed and spewed across the highway. She found a shallow sandy section where she lay on her back and let the water rush over her in a steady stream, so that her tears were taken and mixed with the river. As she lay there, she had a sense of herself dissolving, and no will to resist. It became a kind of ritual she did each day, not planned but instinctual, unable as she was to call upon anything she possessed to wade through this lament.

But this too was a private ritual, hidden from view. She thinks of herself back then, slipped into that gap between the ranges, keeping her grief invisible. A grief as robust as that returned river, but without a rightful place. And she is left with a question: *what is the rightful place of grief?*

Today the congregation came in black and white to pay their respects to the dead. It was something that surprised her when she first arrived here, the way people still dressed so formally for funerals. She'd seen photos of European women clad in black, their faces veiled. But those traditions were changing, in the Catholic Church at least. Funerals were starting to be seen more as celebrations of life, rather than occasions to dwell on death.

The shaved heads, or hair cut short, as a mark of mourning. She'd heard it once said that out here you could measure the distance of death by the length of people's hair, which made it helpful as to how and when you approached them. And these signs of mourning made sense to her now: markers of a rarefied time when the living were close to their dead. It needn't go on forever. But without these signs, mourning was camouflaged, grief concealed.

Months after her brother's funeral, her father had called out of the blue. He rarely rang. They talked about superficial things – her work, his health, the rain. When she asked how he was, his voice faltered. He told her how he'd not been going out much, how he'd withdrawn from people because 'you know, people say strange things sometimes'. He told her how his neighbour, a few weeks after the funeral, had dropped over with a bottle of wine, announcing, 'You've got to get out and start living again!' 'She'd meant well,' he said. Another friend had chased him after church one morning, offering platitudes aplenty when he declined her invitation to morning tea. 'Everything happens for a reason,' she'd concluded with a knowing smile. Amber knew it well, the wisdom dished out at such times. But what is the reason that a child should die? And if you could only find the reason, could things be righted again?

'But why?' her father had said. 'Why not me instead of him?' He went to say something else but his words wouldn't form. They became only sound that stuttered, then stalled. Her father was crying. Outside, a forest of sunflowers had grown in the garden near the door of her flat, had charged up with all the rain. She remembers how their golden brilliance blurred and turned to honey as her own tears came. She'd never known her father to cry. Never heard him say his feelings. Not ever. And now it all seemed too late.

When she was a child, she held onto her father's back while he dived underwater and swam out beyond the breakers. She cannot remember her age. Her small hands gripped his shoulders, careful not to hold too tight around his neck. It is a visceral memory she will never forget, gliding effortlessly through deep water, riding the sea. Her father was a fish, strong and capable in the water.

Tears streamed down her face on the phone to her father that day. But she didn't make a sound, didn't give her own grief away. She had learned this from him. You keep your feelings to yourself, and you do not let others see your weaknesses. She knew he couldn't comfort her. It was her turn to be the parent. She pulled herself together and offered what words she could. She told him to call her anytime. But she felt him fading, wanting to get off the phone. And she let him go.

Of the people who even knew she had a brother, some expressed sorrow, many were kind, some withdrew. She was offered all kinds of wisdoms. About moving on, about gleaning the gold. About being lucky she'd had a chance to say goodbye. But this only made her conceal her sadness, stuff it into her body so it couldn't be seen. She began to avoid being in public, to avoid people altogether, enlisting her dog as her trusted companion.

Often it was strangers, or people Amber knew less well, who made room. Who didn't change the subject when she spoke of the sadness consuming her. Often these people knew death, knew grief. She seized their stories and applied their wisdom like balm. But after a certain time, Amber had the sense that any space granted for mourning had sealed over – it was no longer set aside for her. As if death was an event, an incident, and therefore a milestone that receded while she stumbled forward. As if it wasn't the unbearable weight in all her steps.

Friends advised her to be gentle with herself. But gentleness was no match for what she felt. She needed to wail like those women had wailed. To wring her body of grief. She needed to fall like that woman fell, arms outstretched and flailing. But can you fall if there's no one to catch you, no one to take your weight?

Only the weather was a match for her grief. She let the rains trample her, the lightning fracture her into a thousand pieces, the river roar through her and flush her out. She let herself be taken, and hoped that she might be transformed. The one platitude she'd hung on to was to *give it time*. The idea that time could heal seemed a hopeful belief to adopt. If we kept on living each day, the passing of time would itself be a balm. We need seek no other remedy. Do nothing more.

She tried to make it true, to sit out the grief until it was gone. Like the girl on the high seas, she went about her daily rituals. She collected the mail. Watered the plants. Walked the dog along the river. She continued to work. She needed to be occupied. She stayed on at the community centre for six months, immersing herself in other peoples' troubles. She convinced herself that this helped her put her own loss into perspective, at a time when she needed somewhere to put it. She counselled others through stories of abuse, consoled people heavy with sorrow, drew pictures of family trees so that people might identify family members whose strength might be drawn upon, all the while knowing her own family tree had snapped. Each afternoon, driving home, she felt herself hurtling head-on towards her own grief.

At night, she closed the blinds and cooked. Sometimes she read by the lamplight when she could make her mind stay still. Sometimes she went outside and made a small fire in the backyard with twigs and branches, and sat before it under the stars, waiting for time to heal her. But time didn't seem to pass in this floating village. On and on it went, day after day, round and round. *Night, day; day, night; clouds and flying fish.*

Then that morning with Andrew up on the hill, the morning of the eclipse, before she left town. About to pack up after the pinhole experiment, he asked her how she was going. Amber flinched. It might have been six months, not even. She merely shrugged and continued to pack up. 'My cousin died when I was fifteen,' he said. 'My favourite cousin.'

She felt the urge to interrogate him, as she did with anyone who'd dealt with death, in the hope they might throw her some advice. 'So how did you go on?' she asked.

He was silent for a while before he said, 'I went mad.'

Then he began to pack up and, though it felt abrupt, she was glad to put an end to the conversation.

I went mad. She doesn't know what his madness looked like because she didn't ask. And he didn't say. But she realises now there is not one person, not one thing, that has been said to her this past year more powerful than this. Not because it made her feel better, or gave her comfort, or turned anything around. But it attested that madness was a match for death. That they were an equal force. She has carried his words like a precious note in her pocket, a licence perhaps, to be drawn upon, should she need them. And she feels indebted to him for this.

But how to return? How to restore the taste for life after living so long in the land of the dead? It's been a year. A whole year. Isn't that time enough? She hoped to have moved on by now. She wouldn't have returned had she felt she wasn't ready. And yet in only a few days this place has undone her. She feels impatient. She wants grief gone, for good. How can she make a funeral for her friend?

Travelling blind

Shyanna is drawing with pink chalk on the concrete at Jennifer's house the next morning. Bold circles and shapes. Lines that run the full length of the concrete slab, and have cost her most of the chalk stick, now but a stub in her powdery hand. The marks she makes mirror the ladies' paintings, not in detail so much as style. *She's been watching the women at the art centre,* Amber thinks. Shyanna's face is streaked with pink dust, from where she's wiped the hair from her eyes. When she notices Amber, she pitches the chalk over the edge of the porch and disappears into the doorway darkness. A queue of shopping bags waits against the wall, alongside a stack of freshly primed and stretched canvases.

Jennifer emerges from the house. 'You heading off?'

Amber nods. She has a headache from last night's lack of sleep and is keen to get on the road. She has been caught up here too long. But she wants to see the old lady. She needs to see her. 'Mavis still here?' she asks.

'That old lady out the back. She's painting.'

Amber follows Jennifer around the side of the house. The little timber stumps that the kids had staked their flowers in have all been blown over. The shade cloth draped across the fence is sagging, defeated. Shyanna hurries to retrieve the plastic flowers from the dirt to make her garden again. 'Walpa pulka,' Jennifer says as they pass. '*Big wind* last night.'

Amber is surprised. She hadn't heard the wind with the windows closed at the visitor's centre.

Jennifer shakes her head gravely. At the back of the house she points to the plastic bags caught in the fence and branches, the rubbish cast across the yard. A sheet of corrugated iron has wrapped itself around the red gum. The washing she'd draped on the fence to dry was gone this morning, she says. She'd forgotten about it until she saw it strewn across the neighbours' yard. 'We had to go looking for our things!' Jennifer laughs.

When she tells stories, Jennifer throws her body into the telling, so that she is at once the wind, at once the washing. Shyanna chimes in all the time, sometimes echoing her mother, sometimes embellishing. The storyteller sees she has both the child and the whitefella in her grip, and leads them on. She tells Amber that the family up the street had been sleeping outside and were blown from their beds.

Amber laughs now, incredulous. 'Mulapa?' *Truly?*

'Mulapa.' She nods, trying to keep a straight face. 'Ngaltutjara mulapa!' *Very poor things!*

Whatever wind there was last night is gone. Mavis is sitting outside on a paint-splattered tarp, crossed-legged, her black polyester funeral skirt stretched over her knees. The creases of dust are like lines on a map. Roads and rivers. Beside her, an array of paints and brushes lie waiting. She hasn't yet begun.

Shyanna brings the old lady a canvas from the front porch. She takes it without looking up, then reaches for an empty plastic cup. 'Tjitji!' she interrupts the child, about to settle. She holds the cup out to Shyanna, who skips across the yard and inside to fill it with water. Amber notices a tremor in the old lady's outstretched hand. 'You should sit down,' Mavis says, throwing her chin towards the ground in front of her. There is something queenly about this lady, and Amber does as she's told. Jennifer goes inside. Mavis reaches for a stick, begins to poke at the coals. Shyanna settles beside Amber, wriggling to get comfortable, a narrow strip of canvas offcut before her.

It has already been painted on, but she begins to prime it as she has seen the old ladies do. To begin again.

Amber sees she cannot ask for anything after all. Mavis is not the ngangkari today. She is the artist. She is embarrassed to have thought of bothering her. What she felt she needed she can't even say, and what she thought the old lady could possibly give her seems silly now, in the light of day.

The artist starts by peeling the plastic cling wrap off the paint-encrusted cups, scrunching each in her fist, then letting it fall to the ground. Swiftly a dog appears, sniffs at the discarded balls of plastic, then sidles over to collapse in the sun. The old lady starts her painting with a practical air, as if preparing vegetables for dinner. But soon she leans forward, her back low and rounded. A mop of silver curls falls forward like springs, almost scraping the canvas. Sprouts of grey beard bubble on her chin like steel wool. As she makes the first marks with the selected brush she starts to sing, quietly at first, as if to herself. Like in the car the other night. She continues like this for some time, painting and singing. It is like being privy to some private ceremony, and Amber finds herself falling into reverent composure. Then suddenly Mavis throws back her head, looks at Amber and laughs, that high-pitched single-note shriek of a laugh that belongs to the ladies out here and never fails to disarm. She turns the painting, then, without pause, launches back into her song.

So her stories go. Stories that drift into song as they meander through the landscape. Stories that reach down like roots into this country, are bound to it. Stories a traveller might stuff in her pockets and take with her. Stories to fill you up, that might keep you from getting hungry somewhere down the track. Each stanza punctuated by a gasping breath. And every now and then the storyteller returns to her audience, checks that Amber is listening. 'Kulini?' *Are you taking it in?*

Is she taking it in? How much detail will be lost on this whitefella as her remembering skims the surface, gleaning only the shiny things on the road? Gleaning, straining, gathering and, even then, interpreting. Trying to fit it into a framework she already holds. Despite how long she's lived in this country, she is still the traveller, with a traveller's myopic lens. Always passing through. No matter that she has come to know some of the communities, the country out here, still she cannot conceive of the detail the old lady talks about. Or any one place, perhaps. Part of her is impatient, anxious to distance herself from this place and the events of yesterday. To shift camp before the shadow of death once more descends.

But she is listening. She is trying to comprehend as much as she can with her elementary language, language she's neither heard nor spoken in years. Language rendered obsolete each time she leaves this country, left rattling around in her pocket like old money – beautiful and exotic, but without currency. Here language unlocks the country, illuminates its detail – the ecology, the history, the mythology bound to it. She stretches herself to understand, so that it feels like her whole being, with all of her senses, is reaching towards the old woman's words. Occasionally Mavis switches to English, to emphasise something for Amber's benefit, but as she does Amber hears the hollows in the story, sites of dropped detail.

Everything is still, as if time itself has stood still, for a bit. The sun is warm. The sky unbroken blue. Two camp dogs doze limply by the front door, but for the occasional flick of a jaw when the flies become too persistent. A trail of ants follows some cartographic trail across the ground, like an old bush track that can no longer be seen but can nevertheless be followed by those who remember it. Up the street, voices rise and fall, go quiet for a bit, then erupt in a chorus of alternating cheers and sighs, over and over. Must be gambling.

Mavis builds her painting like a topographic map, in thick accretions of acrylic. It is the same painting, always the same painting. Her country. When the old lady talks, it is as if sometimes she is drawing stories from the country around them, and at other times from herself. Looking out, then in, to a map Amber cannot see. As if the country is inside her, animating her. Every now and then she looks up from her work and traces the distant hills with the tip of the brush. As if she is painting a landscape, but she is not. She squints her eyes like she's seeing right through the country, into its guts. She is speaking not of what is apparent but of what has transpired here, the events that brought this country into being. She talks about a time past and mythic, yet present in the physical landscape. It's a way of seeing impossible for Amber to really comprehend. But what she can see, although she couldn't see when she first came here, is that the country is alive with stories. And she knows this now of everywhere.

'Nyaratja.' *Over there.* Mavis sees that the whitefella's gaze is general, unfocused, and shakes her head. 'Wiya!' *No!* She points again with the paintbrush tip, through a copse of trees to a series of quartz rocks protruding from the earth. 'Nyaratja – that one.' Place is precise.

This is what is lost when people pass. This precision, this detail. Family maps, community maps, maps of country. They take it with them when they go. Without its stories, Amber wonders, will the country be mute? And the rest of us – will we be but wayfarers travelling blind?

The old lady sits back, straightens up, surveys the work. 'Palya.' She is not finished, but she is finished with her audience. It occurs to Amber that these paintings are maps of sorts. Records of country that reach beyond landscape. Perhaps this is what is being left us, after all. Then, when she's about to get up, Mavis reaches to touch Amber's hand, her paintbrush still poised between her fingers. 'Ananyi?' *Are you going?* Amber hesitates. 'Ngaltutjara,' the old lady says, tilting her head to the side. 'You been lost your spirit,' she whispers.

Words rise inside her. Rise and fall. To open her mouth is to risk the waters rushing out. Waters that writhe with monsters and ugly beasts. That threaten to drown her. Like the child of the high seas, who couldn't cry out despite her desperate desire to do so. When she tried her throat closed up and no sound came, the effort so intense it caused her face and throat to blacken, like the face of someone drowned. Apart from one day, when a cargo-boat appeared, sailing effortlessly over the watery streets and sounding its siren. This time, the village did not disappear, nor was the girl overcome by sleep. On this occasion, the child recognised the sound from the world she once knew, and rushed to the window, crying out with all her might: 'Help! Help!'

But Amber didn't cry out. Water brimmed in her eyes, like waves that would not break. *You been lost your spirit.* A diagnosis is almost enough.

It is told that the Heliades wept day and night for four months by the grave of their dead brother. That their wasting bodies took root and were soon encrusted in bark, their arms turned to branches. Even so, their tears still flowed. But they hardened in the sun, like honey turned to stone. Is this what it means to have lost one's spirit? To move through the world each day but have no taste for it? To no longer be able to feel its touch, or receive its offerings? Could the ngangkari see right through her, into the woody forest that flourished there?

'I was going to ask . . .' Amber begins, then falters.

No Stones, No Wood

The old lady reaches for Amber's arm and draws her gently down. Without a word, she rotates her body and levers her hands up under Amber's shirt, placing them firmly on her back. Slowly she starts to rub in large circular motions. Amber closes her eyes as massive hands knead her skin. No, deeper than skin. These hands knead through her skin. As if her hands have eyes, can see her, shift her this way and that. On and on it goes. This woman who seems to move so roughly through the world, like it doesn't matter, has the smoothest hands. Not like silk. Like stone that's been a long time tumbling in water. The repetition of the rubbing, the old lady's deep and steady breath, the sun – all make it hard to stay awake.

'You been lost your spirit, must be.' Now the old lady's words punch the dammed-up grief inside her. Amber tries to hold herself together, filled with feelings of embarrassment and shame. She has never cried in front of anyone. And she has never lost her composure in all these years coming here. Like other whitefellas, her role has been to fix things, to manage things, to make herself invisible. To help people, not to ask for help herself. But the force is too great.

Sadness rushes through her like rain, until, unable to resist, she becomes it. She is the river come down, banks collapsed and flowing now, a torrent of clay-coloured foam and latte-like froth. Scouring out the sand and silt and dredging up the rubbish. Nothing is spared. Not the broken glass nor the beer cans, the plastic nappies and the discarded clothing now bloated and floating like ghosts. Here it is, all thrown together, lurching forward in full flow. Her mother's shoulders crumbling; her father's broken voice on the phone. Her sick brother who can't stand up. Who says, 'I've got to be able to walk,' and then falls down. The woman from the funeral who collapses, sobbing with grief, and the child of the high seas who screams, with a strangled voice, 'Help! Help!'

Then a wave came to find her. This wave was extremely independent and had hitherto kept a distance from the village. It was a large wave and could spread out on either side much further than any other. In its crest it carried two seeming eyes of foam. It was as though it could see and understand certain things, without always approving. Although it formed and broke many hundred times a day, it never forgot to furnish itself afresh with these two eyes, always set in exactly the same position and very life-like. Sometimes, when the wave's attention was taken by something interesting, it might be found resting for a whole minute together, its crest in the air, its function of wave that made it necessary to break and remake every seven seconds completely forgotten.

For a long time this wave had wanted to do something for the child, without exactly knowing what. The wave saw the cargo-boat sail off into the distance and understood very well the agony of the one who was left behind. Keeping aloof no longer, it drew the child a little way off, without any word being spoken, and as though leading her by the hand.

After kneeling in front of the child, in the manner of waves, and with the very greatest reverence, it rolled the child in its depths, pressed her there for one long moment, seeking, with the help of death, to snatch the child from her unhappiness. And to help the wave in this grave task, the child stopped breathing.

But the end did not come; so the wave threw the child high in the air, tossed her easily, as though she were no bigger than a sea-swallow, caught and recaught her like a ball, till she fell back at last among foam flakes big as the eggs of an ostrich.

At last, seeing that nothing could come of all this, that it could not succeed in bringing death to the child, the wave, in an immense murmur of tears and apologies, carried her back home.

Then it is finished. Unceremoniously, almost abruptly, it is finished. Amber feels the warmth of the hands withdraw, cold air prickle her skin. She feels the edge of the old lady's body beside her, like a row of tiny hooks and eyes, unclasped one by one. In the past year, Amber has been unable to be this close to anyone. She breathes in, exhales. Opens her eyes. So much sunlight. Mavis beside her like a mother on the edge of the bed. 'You be right now.' Her manner is matter-of-fact. And for a moment Amber lets herself believe that grief can be pulled off like a bandaid from a child's knee. *All better now.* She has nothing but a shirt sleeve to dry her face, her streaming nose. 'You be right now,' the old lady repeats in the kindest tone. Then again, getting up, 'You be right now.' And they both smile as the sweet sound of Shyanna's singing announces her presence.

So that's how it goes. Nothing extracted – no stones, no wood. Nothing to hold in her palm, nor throw to the wind. Nothing to bottle or bury. But inside the sea is calm. The wind has dropped.

At the very last house, on the outskirts of the community, a mob of children are jumping high on a trampoline, like springs to the sky. Broken bikes and plastic toys are strewn around the yard, as if they've been washed up on the night tide. The children's laughter and screams ring out, amplify the silence that follows. As she drives away, Amber feels inside a small shift she recognises as hope. She has to hold onto it.

UPSIDE DOWN

She has lost two days, and still has a day's driving ahead of her. How she came to be there, in the first place, it is hard to think. Because of the family who asked for a ride home from the football? Because of the song of the old lady who rocked to and fro on the back seat of the car that night? Or was it the sleeping child, eyes opening now and then like pools of ink? Time has turned on its head in this otherworld, or slowed like it might in some kind of myth or fairytale. *Time did not pass in the floating village.* Or is it that time no longer holds weight or meaning? She only left town two days ago. But if this is the case, how long will two weeks take?

On the seat beside her lies the painting Shyanna gave her just before she left. A fairytale map, perhaps, with no key to decode it? All blues and pinks and yellows. 'Which way up?' Amber had asked as she held it up, delighted. The little girl shrugged, Silly question. What did it matter? She had seen many artists out here turn the canvas around while they worked. The orientation didn't seem important.

When they moved to the city, her brother had begun to draw upside down. She knows this to be precisely when it started because his first upside-down drawings showed the city skyline, which could be seen across the river from their new house. At first her mother thought these 'long buildings', as he called them, which looked as if they were submerged in the river, were reflections. But soon she saw how all of his drawings needed to be reversed in order to read them. People with legs in the air, houses balanced on the ridgelines of their roofs, trees with tendril-like roots seeking the sky. Amber started watching him draw more studiously. He would start his people with eyes, always big, round eyes, then the mouth would appear above, and up they would go from there.

If her mother was concerned she didn't show it. She simply turned each drawing the right way around upon completion. Like his teachers, she was in awe of his skill, and it was for this reason that she showed the new artworks to their father. But their father was concerned about the need for reorientation. His reaction was disquieting and their mother recoiled. Perhaps it flared her own lack of confidence. Had she not noticed something was wrong with her child? Her brother was consequently carted off to a doctor, who thankfully assured their mother that it was most likely a phase, though usually seen in children younger than him. It would likely pass, he said.

Perhaps their father took this as a defeat of his own position, for he showed little interest in his son's work after this. It bothered him to a degree Amber couldn't understand. He wanted all things to be right, even his children. Or maybe it was more a concern that his son showed no sign of leaving art behind. He seemed to spend much more time on art than anything else. He wasn't into sport, like most boys. He dutifully played rugby each Saturday only because he wasn't given any choice. He rode his bike and climbed trees. He read. But mostly he made art.

She is not sure how long this lasted, maybe only a couple of years. Like her mother, Amber accepted the orientation of her brother's art. But now she wonders what was happening for him. He was nine when they left the cattle station. He hadn't wanted to go. Amber was young enough to be seduced by the idea of the city, but it was harder for him. He belonged to that place. Like an animal adapted to a particular habitat, it was nearly impossible to imagine his survival elsewhere.

Her mother would sit on the edge of his bed in those months before they left. She used to come at night to say prayers with them before sleep. Three Hail Marys, one Our Father and half an apple each – this was their bedtime ritual. They learned their prayers by heart because, their mother told them, 'You never know when you might need them. You might not always be able to find words.'

It was an abstract idea and out of reach, but Amber loved learning prayers, whatever the point of them. It was like learning songs. She had her own prayers as well, which she would whisper under the blankets when her mother left the room. A call to God to look after her family and keep them safe. She couldn't go to sleep without saying them.

Her mother's voice was steady those nights, steering. 'There's a river and hills where you can ride your bike,' she told them. 'You'll have your own bedroom.' But her brother remained quiet. He wanted to take his collections with him.

As kids, they spent hours fossicking through abandoned rubbish dumps on the cattle station, bowers of piled-up bits and pieces left by those who lived there before them. They scratched around like chooks, searching for precious things. Old irons and kettles, a butter churn once, a number of partially buried bottles, mottled with thread-like webs of earth. So strange it felt to hold objects once held by others, since passed. Common things exalted by being out of context, out of time.

Whether they were going in search of findings or simply walking to the cattle yards or the shed, her brother would always turn something up. Amber was envious of his ability to see things and strained to do the same. But while she overlooked a rock, her brother would roll it over, and more often than not a skinny lizard would shoot out, or a nest of woodlice would be exposed. While her eyes were glued to the track on their way to the windmill, in the hope that something would appear at her feet, he'd pluck an eagle feather snared on the barbed-wire fence, or extract a piece of fluorescent orange fungus from a fencepost with his penknife.

He would say of a feather, 'Look what a bird left for me!' Always like that. 'The hens have laid eggs for us!' he would announce, his palms a palette of freshly laid eggs, some brown, some speckled, some the colour of fresh cream. It made them feel extra special, these gifts from the chickens. It made you turn them in your hands as you placed them carefully in the fridge, and feel the variations of size and weight and colour. As if everything chanced upon had been left there to find. As if the world was ceaselessly offering things.

Her mother helped him decide the things that might be parted with. 'We can't take the bones from under the house. It's best to leave those behind. But we can take the boards with butterfly wings, and all the feathers and stones and things you've found.'

'How about the bottles?'

'You can take the bottles.'

'How about the snake?'

The snake her brother wanted to bring was the one their father had shot in the shed one day when they'd been playing cowboys. Her brother had saddled up the timber saw benches with their father's saddles, and they had only just mounted when Amber noticed he was motionless. He was staring at the rafters. 'It's a brown snake,' her brother said very slowly, without turning to her. 'Get down.'

Amber had managed to slide off one side of the leather saddle, her leg trembling as her foot touched the ground. But her other foot got stuck in the stirrup, so that as she pulled it over, the saddle capsized over the side of the bench. The snake's head moved and she started screaming. As she did she could hear her brother saying, 'Give me the saddle – just give me the saddle,' but it was as if the screaming set off a kind of terror inside her, which made her scream even more. She couldn't take her eyes off that snake.

It was her screams that brought their father running from the house. She remembers the figure framed by the shed door, rifle in hand. The gunshot that silenced her screaming. The smell of horse and sulphur, leather and oil. The saddle on the ground, her foot still tangled in the stirrup. Like a trapped rabbit.

Her father moved towards her, rifle in hand. 'I told you kids not to touch my things.' There followed one single thump between her shoulders. The same blow ricochets in her body each time she recalls this moment, the physical shock inseparable from the shock that the one who had come to save them from the snake was the one who bit them in the end. His anger concealed any concern he might have felt. He offered no comfort to his children.

With one arm her father scooped the saddle up from the ground and swung it onto an iron hook. Her brother got what her father called 'a clip over the ear', a quick, sharp hit to the side of the head. As they trailed behind him up to the house, the rifle limp at his side, Amber wished she'd been bitten and rushed to hospital, maybe even died, so her father was riddled with guilt.

But her brother was thinking about that snake. Once their father left the house, having returned the rifle to its keeping place under her parents' bed, the first thing her brother said to their mother was, 'Do you think he'll let me keep it?' Amber wondered if the worst part of the incident for him was losing any negotiating power he might have had to keep the carcass. Though they'd encountered many snakes on the cattle station, her brother didn't yet have any in his collection – at least, not whole. He had skins and skeletons in various states of completeness, but he was always on the lookout for pristine remains.

He'd wanted the body of the brown snake that had slipped across the linoleum in the kitchen only weeks before, which their mother had clubbed with the back of a broom and banished from the house with one powerful sweep. Amber and her brother had hung over the back railing in their pyjamas and watched in awe while their father hacked off its head with a shovel on the grass to finish it off. He'd thrown the carcass over the fence into the paddock. The next day she and her brother had landed like vultures to investigate the corpse, made inferior in her brother's mind because of the decapitation.

It was their mother who negotiated the deal for her brother to save the snake shot in the shed. She'd suggested preserving it, as if it was her own idea. And so that snake was pickled in methylated spirits and parked on the shelf at the head of her brother's bed. When they journeyed to the city it travelled with them in the back seat, the glass jar wedged between her brother's feet, along with whatever other artefacts from his collection he had crammed into the car. Their father would gladly have left behind her brother's strange assembly of things.

What they didn't take with them her brother captured in pencil and ink, documenting the excavation site under the house, preserving insects and bird bones on paper. He had seen similar illustrations in a book he'd borrowed from the town library, with fine lines that led to the scientific names of specimens.

At their new house, he reconstructed the remains of his collection in a small square room at the end of the closed-in verandah, which they called 'the sleep-out'. Their mother managed to find a couple of chests with drawers in second-hand shops, and her brother laid his boards inside them, pinned with petrified insects and exoskeletons, the fragile bones of birds and mice. Reconfigured in the new world, these objects became the potent and precious records of the country from which they'd come.

Amber's bedroom was at the other end of the sleep-out, separated from her brother's by a strip of glass louvres, which opened out onto a backyard that tumbled down at a steep decline to the back fence. Her mother painted the walls of the sleep-out a garish green that sung of the seventies. Amber's bedroom was sunflower-yellow. It was much bigger than the one she had once shared with her brother, but she didn't like being on her own. She often found herself hovering at her brother's doorway, waiting for an invitation into his cabinet of curiosities. If the door was closed, she'd play between the rooms, so that soon her belongings spilled from her bedroom, making a trail towards her brother's door.

The street where her family came to live was on a hill above the river, houses clinging like barnacles exposed at low tide, with roofs of terracotta tile and corrugated iron. After school she would go with her brother to a small park at the top of the hill and swing on the fence where the wire mesh was torn open, hook her knees around the steel bar and dangle upside down to look across at the city. At dusk the lights would glitter like jewels, full of promise.

The city of their everyday was more like a sea of houses. The streets were steep and mostly crooked, winding their way around the hills and saddles of the suburb. She and her brother would climb and clatter down them at full speed on their dragsters, slowly absorbing the map of the new world that would soon be marked on them indelibly. At once a street directory, at once a mud map etched out by the kids of the area as they explored the off-road pathways, the back lanes, the parks, and made meeting places and markers of street corners. They climbed the maze of giant jacaranda and poinsettia branches which lined the street, and looked out, like sailors scaling ships' masts, across the ocean of red and purple flowers, interrupted only by rooftops, to the river.

Up and down and around the streets they dragged their bikes. They congregated at the shut-down petrol station on the corner of the main road at the bottom of the hill, which for years remained vacant. It was a prime meeting place for the kids of the neighbourhood, carpeted with overripe mangoes that rotted on the summer concrete, emitting a sweet, dank smell. Amber reaches back to recover this world again, but sees how place, once departed, can never again be solid. What was once home is now a series of amorphous shapes, of light and shadow and fleeting movement, all of it laced with longing.

Her brother recorded the new world with pencil and ink, albeit upside down. Houses perched on stilts, verandahs wrapped around, adorned with hanging plants and stairs that spilt into grassy yards. Some were contained by timber fences but many were not, so that the kids could empty out of one house and into another without checkpoints.

By the time he was in high school, her brother's art was winning prizes – school prizes, state prizes. Mostly drawings, in charcoal, lead and ink. Sometimes he painted with acrylic. Even then he went back over his paintings, adding detail in lead, sometimes scrawls of text. Landscapes. Always landscapes. The folds and creases of distant hills formed by lines and light. The crumpled surface of a river luminescent in the afternoon sun. Later, the grain of the sea where he came to live, expressed through strokes and smudges of black ink.

Even figures, human and animal, were depicted as landscapes, now she thinks of it. One of her favourites was a herd of wild horses running against a landscape that could be seen through their bodies, so that the sinews and bones of the brumbies became indistinguishable from the textures of the trees, the hills, the ground. She once read a critic talking about the *density* of his work, and she thought how beautifully apt the choice of words. This is how her brother saw the world – dense, detailed. Each mark he made on paper reflected this.

Even now, to look at his work is to be again the little sister trailing along beside him, having stones turned up, insects uncovered from the leaf litter. Perhaps the artist and the collector are one and the same. Each a bowerbird of a kind, picking and plucking and preserving the things which, if reassembled, recover the world. Perhaps the orientation doesn't matter.

Return to dust

Two or three lit windows checker the night canvas as she drives into the quiet community. Otherwise the houses are dark, huddled. She calls to them but they remain silent. She loops around, trying to find Emma's house. The Toyota's engine burdens the silence.

Amber is told about the young man by a Maori fellow, tattooed arm hanging like a fish hook out the window of his ute. He does not look at her when he speaks. 'Hung himself in a tree. Just swingin'.' He tilts his head back towards the main road. 'Had to cut him down. That stump now. Knew that tree had to go.'

She remembers seeing, on the side of the road that brought her in, a memorial in place of that tree. A small white cross jutted out of a severed stump. Plastic flowers woven through the wire that fenced it off. How the synthetic colours had sung against their washed-out surrounds, had stung the faded grasses. In the last light.

Only the camp dogs are out, scrounging the streets for scraps. Everyone is gone to the sorry camp in the neighbouring community. A whole community up and gone, to set up camp somewhere else. There's a lightness to this that isn't hers. Blowing in the wind, backwards and forwards, in a call and response to what life dishes out.

The Maori fellow points her to Emma's house. As she pulls in, Emma appears at the door, silhouetted by the inside light. She walks into the car light. Inside, Emma tells Amber that it looks unlikely they will be running the holiday camp after all. Amber had known about the death, but with the funeral delayed, owing to a conflict in the community, people had maintained it would be good to provide something for the kids to do. They were happy for them to take some of the young people out, to get them away for a bit. But apparently the issue has been resolved and the funeral is going ahead. They will get the final word tomorrow.

The kitchen table is strewn with single sheets of ruled paper, scrawled with black ink handwriting. On the floor a large map, with curling sides, is weighted in each corner by one object or another. A boot, a book, a water bottle. Emma's partner, Ben, is typing, his right hand on the keyboard of his laptop, left hand reaching over to his papers. Like he's trying to hold things in place lest he lose his bearings. He presses the fourth corner of the map flat on the floor with his bare foot but still the paper recoils against the weights, resistant.

Ben barely acknowledges Amber's arrival, apart from a quick sideways glance, a fraction of a smile. But when Emma starts to dish out dinner, he moves to get up. 'Sorry, I can move my stuff.'

'No, don't worry. We can sit in the lounge.' Emma takes two plates of curry into the lounge, and Amber follows. 'He's trying to finish a report,' she tells Amber. 'It's due in a few days.'

Ben looks relieved and sits back down. 'Sorry. I hope you don't mind if I'm a bit anti-social?'

When Amber finishes her meal she is ready for bed. But come nightfall, a terrible chorus of starving dogs starts up, howling and snapping to the sky. She lies awake for a long time, despite her exhaustion, before she presses her face against the window grille and lets out a guttural growl. What seems like a thousand dogs shoot like spears through the spinifex. In the interval of quiet that follows she tries to sleep, but it isn't long before a piercing bark splits the night and the chorus starts up again.

When she wakes the next day, Emma is gone. Ben is working at the kitchen table again, as if he hasn't been to sleep. The smell of toast and coffee lingers. 'Dogs not wake you up?' he says. He stands and walks towards the back door. 'I think that's a puppy now.'

Amber realises that the yelping is now coming from a single animal. When they open the door, several dogs are queued on the doorstep, silently waiting. They do not plead. They lower their heads like humble street beggars. *Lord, have mercy on us.* The yelping puppy catapults towards them. They shut the door in time.

When Amber goes for a shower outside, the puppy follows her, then disappears behind the shower block. Amber walks around the building to find a bitch lying down, a dead pup draped by her side. Ben brings a shovel and they bury the puppy outside the back fence. But within half an hour the mother has dug it up. She tucks it into the arc of her empty belly like a foetus, while her other pup, riddled with lice, runs hungry. The slightest of movements inside the house triggers the desperate yelping of the puppy. But if they feed one, what might they start? There might be a hundred dogs in this place that, on smelling the scent of food, might tear each other apart.

By midmorning Emma is still not back from the sorry camp in the neighbouring community. Ben continues to work at the table. Amber feels in the way. She would like to go for a walk, to leave the house, but she's stopped by the dogs, and by what has happened here. And she knows well enough that you can't walk around without permission. She doesn't know this community. She goes to the lounge room and tries to begin a book, but finds herself reading the same sentences over and over.

She's relieved when Ben offers her a coffee, and she comes into the kitchen. He places her cup on the table, as if inviting her to sit down. She can't help glancing at the sketchy diagrams. 'Is it okay to look?'

'Nothing sensitive here,' he says. 'Just family trees.'

She sips her coffee. Names arranged in schematics of trees, generations stacked one on top of the other. Circles and squares to indicate gender. Arrows shooting out to the margins, with handwriting at all angles. Some words underlined, some crossed out. *Just family trees.* Lines on a page that link us to the past, to each other. Lines as flimsy and as tight as thread that can reach across countries, across oceans, across time, tugging us together into lineages, which might pull and fray and even snap, leaving gaps and question marks on the page.

Her grandmother was the keeper of the family tree. Her exquisite handwriting, her snow-white hair, permed in her later years into soft, full curls. Blue eyes, her grandmother had. She always wore blue. Amber can't remember her in any other colour. Blue beads about her neck, blue clip-on earrings. 'Any colour as long as it's blue,' she used to say in a sing-song way. Blue skirts, blue shirts, blue eyes like stones.

She tended the family tree by telling stories, tracing each of them back through time to instil in her family a sense of inheritance. She was the first person Amber knew to have this role, or the first person through which she came to understand its importance. Grandma could tell endless stories of so-and-so's mother and how she was connected to what's-his-name. She turned up surnames like stones to recover maiden names and trace who married whom and when and where they lived.

So that soon you were forced to make a map in your head to keep up. And over time Amber realised that she, too, must have figured in 'Grandma's stories'. That as her grandmother went about connecting the people in her life, she was also being mapped into a particular genealogy, located in a family story. When they lost their grandmother, they lost this map, because none of it was written down.

'Looks like a puzzle,' she comments.

Ben comes over and sits back down, sighing. 'Still a few missing pieces. This bloke's so confusing,' he says, and taps a lead pencil on one name. 'Turns out he had three fathers. His biological father, then two other fathers who grew him up. The name on this genealogy is actually two of his fathers' names merged together.'

'So it's a mistake?'

'Took me a while to work it out. But he identified with the countries of all three fathers.'

As Ben speaks, it is as if he is simply saying his thoughts aloud rather than inviting dialogue, like he's rolling the information around in the palm of his hand. Once finished, he continues to enter data. Amber envies his purpose. She returns to the lounge and takes up her book again.

She remembers how she lingered at her brother's door, wanting in on his magical world of things. Rows of butterflies and bugs pinned to ink-blue velvet, wings splayed. Dragonflies suspended in bottles of alcohol laced with coloured dye. Dried specimens meticulously labelled and arranged by species. Everything ordered, everything in its place. Perhaps Ben's work is something of the same. The work of putting things together, putting people together, placing them side by side. Things that belong to one another. Creating connections, making patterns, ordering the vastness. The dull click of the keyboard is strangely soothing.

Outside, the wind picks up again. It sweeps through the valley, rattling the louvres and smacking the saplings against the side of the house. Through unsealed windows and under doors it tries desperately to break in. The pressure produces an unrelenting, high-pitched whine. Rubbish bins are blown over, emptied out, and disposable nappies, plastic bottles, chip packets strewn across the streets. Inside, Amber takes refuge, waits for it to be done. This wind has come to clear the spirits out, she tells herself.

Under her feet, a thin film of dust masks the scuffed linoleum. She sweeps it out. Later she will sweep it out again. How long would it take for the desert to reclaim these houses, she wonders, should we surrender our brooms?

All morning the abandoned houses moan in the dry wind. Then suddenly they fall silent with its passing, leaving a hush like nothing has happened. Amber goes to the back door. For a moment, the sound of unpeopled places, unlived-in kitchens, empty beds. Then the dogs again, whimpering, wandering over. She shuts them out.

House by the Sea

When Emma returns, it is as expected. Things have turned around. Tomorrow Amber will drive back to town and this crazy journey will come to an end. She feels a mix of relief and frustration. But there's nothing can be done for now.

But this place isn't done with her yet. Come night, dreams dig up her own dead, drag in things from the past. Half-digested things. Her brother's eyes wake her. Jet-black eyes, made dull by the morphine he was taking to numb the pain in those last weeks. Eyes made huge by hollowed-out cheeks, the confusion at what was happening. This is the clearest picture Amber has seen of his face, or let in, for a long time.

Sleeplessness stretches the night into immeasurable distances, with no road stops, no rest areas ahead. She turns like a boat on a troubled sea. Waters she has been avoiding tug and tumble her.

She is carried back to her brother's house by the sea. He'd moved there once he'd stopped work. There was no real point in staying in the city. He never liked the city. He used to escape to the island whenever he could. Moving there meant moving further away from medical treatment, but for him it was more important to be in a place he loved, and it was only a ferry ride away.

Amber had gone back to be with him in those last weeks. He'd wanted to stay home til the end. People came and went – uncles, aunts, a handful of friends. Her parents visited separately. All of them wanting to be close to him, to comfort him in any way they could. Looking back, she sees how gracious Claire was to let them do what they needed in that little house. But still she'd felt in the way, unable to be as useful as she needed to be.

Her mother sweeping. From the inside, slowly she would make her way out, around the deck that skirted the front of the timber house. Sometimes someone else would start this only a few hours later. Or mop the floors again, until they squeaked. The bath was bleached so white it glared. The towels were washed and folded and folded again. One day Amber came back from a walk to find the house flooded with light. Her mother had decided to take the curtains down and wash them. Sunlight streamed in, startled them like animals in their dark burrow. In the afternoons it washed in from the west, pressing against the plate glass so that they were forced to the other side of the house. In her memory, the house on those days was tilted like a boat, all of them tipped to one side together, away from the windows. But that can't be true.

Anything left on a surface was quickly put away, so that after a while it was hard for Amber not to feel part of the clutter. She became uncertain whether there was room for her. She made a camp in the backyard, between the house and the garden studio, pitched a tent at the base of a scribbly gum. At night the air was electric with the sound of crickets, but underneath, in the distance, the lullaby of the sea.

The studio was closed. Shut up like someone had gone on holiday. The timber blinds were pulled so you couldn't see in. Claire had offered it as a place for her to sleep, but she couldn't sleep in there. It was his place. House of his things. On the small timber deck at the back door, cuttlefish bones were stacked in little cairns. Trays of bones, bleached in peroxide, laid out in rows. The skeletons of birds and lizards and fish found on the island. They made her happy and sad all at once.

At their house in the country, her brother had kept his bone collection under the house. It had been relegated there after the bones were discovered by her mother, and thankfully not her father, in a curtained-off chamber under the desk in the bedroom they shared. The collection was mainly comprised of cattle bones he'd cleaned and polished and horns he'd found around the station, but also the fine-boned skulls of birds, the skeletons of mice. Once a complete bird skeleton, its wings fully articulated, like fans.

The bones he painstakingly scrubbed with an old toothbrush and laid out to dry on wooden pallets. In a museum they would have been accompanied by text that said the collection referenced the years of drought that would ultimately lead to their leaving. Paddocks littered in decaying carcasses as they drove out of that country. Hides torn back to bone, white as teeth. Open burials in the browning earth.

They'd tried to reconstruct a complete skeleton once, but soon abandoned the task, opting instead to build a strange beast from what bones they had. Her brother snaffled some craft glue from school and this they used to bind their specimen together. But the weight of the bones soon depleted their short supply of glue. They tried wiring them and had some success, but in the end they decided to mount them directly upon the soil, creating what they thought looked like an authentic archaeological dig. They were pleased with this change of direction. They fancied the idea of others finding the site long after they'd gone, believing it to hold the remains of some unknown beast embedded in the soil.

When they came to the city, her brother continued to collect bones, but more so that he could draw them. After he left school, while his friends were out running amok, he'd be at the museum, sketching from display cases. Finally, he managed to get access to the archives, where he spent his days slumped over open drawers, sketching the fragile skeletons of small mammals and reptiles in lead. He returned to the use of actual bones many years later, in his sculptures. Snake vertebrae as petals in a brooch's flower. In recent years he'd asked Amber to bring camel bones in her suitcase, which he carved into delicate paper knives.

It was upsetting to see the bones outside the studio, exposed to the elements, gathering dust. Her brother had told Claire not to touch them, that he would get back to them. Amber looked for signs on her sister-in-law's face as to whether or not she believed this, or whether she was just going along with it. It felt like a kind of deceit. Amber had never hidden anything from her brother. But to pack his things away before he was gone would have felt an act of trespass.

But this is not what upset her most that day. When she'd gone to live in the desert, her brother had told her about a fossil site he'd read about a few hours from town. He'd wanted to come and camp out with her, to draw the bones of the megafauna they'd been excavating from the earth for several years. But things always seemed to get in the way. 'Next winter,' they'd say each year, as if another winter was something to be taken for granted. Ten years had passed. When Amber saw the bones laid out on the studio verandah during that final visit, she was struck by the fact that his winters had run out. Time had run out. They would never do this together.

Behind her camp in the garden, the hills hoist. Washing on the wire, coming in, going out. *Night, day; day, night.* Baskets of laundry placed in the lounge and quickly distributed to bedrooms, before the basket was empty again. When they weren't doing housework, they hovered around in a kind of waiting room, whispering to one another. Barely daring to touch the timber floor, lest somebody wake him. Like the house of a sleeping baby. They were not really able to say what it was they were waiting for, nor able to begin the grieving they all felt coming. Like grey clouds gathering, their very presence signalled a storm.

She thinks now how careful they all were with each other, how careful and how checked. She, her mother and her sister-in-law going over and over the medication her brother was using, timing the doses, reporting symptoms as they appeared. As if the right combination of drugs, or the right equation of food and sunlight, might hold things steady. Even reverse things. But things were not steady. Her brother was in terrible pain, and anything that could quell his suffering would also sedate his spirit, holding him in a kind of halfway house, a liminal space between life and death.

As she lies awake Amber traces time backwards. Things had gone so fast. Only a year before that final visit, they'd sat together at the coffee table her brother had made, Claire's handmade coffee cups before them. Her brother had salvaged an old printer's tray from an antique market, which he'd turned into an inlay for a tabletop, a glass sheet covering the drawer of miniature wooden cases. Inside was a small-scale museum of found and cherished objects collected over the years. Shells, buttons, shafts of stone. Rusted keys, coins, glass blunted by the sea. Some things reached back to the cattle station of their childhood – a piece of orange fungus he'd found, a collection of marbles crammed into one tiny compartment, letter tiles from the family Scrabble set.

It was on that previous visit that her brother had gone to get up and lost his balance. Amber moved to help him but he'd steadied himself on the back of the chair, taken a few deep breaths, then sat back down again. 'I've got to be able to do this,' he said. 'I've got to be able to walk!' Then he tried again to pull himself up. But his body was shaking. He couldn't do it. He couldn't *walk*.

Her sister-in-law was standing outside on the deck, her back to them. One hand resting on the timber railing, pale blue paint peeling. She was wearing a floral dress with a mint-green background, splashes of pink and teal and black. She either couldn't hear what was happening inside or she had seen it already and was letting Amber see, letting her know. In the moments that followed, Amber watched through the sliding glass doors while the wind lifted Claire's cotton dress and let it fall, so that it sucked against her legs, which stood as strong and still as a trunk, tanned from a life in the sun. She watched Claire's dark hair being whipped about. Her failure to smooth it down, to tame it.

That afternoon Amber left the house. Crossed the street and walked up the road for a bit, to where a clearing in the dense vegetation marked the start of a sandy track down to the beach. The local beach was not patrolled and often rough. But this meant they often had it to themselves. They'd been coming here since they were kids, when they'd walk from beach to beach between headlands, all the way around to the point. Sometimes they'd swim in the shallows, but mostly they'd explore the rocks that rimmed the shoreline, encrusted in barnacles and blue polished periwinkles, with sponges, anemones and other tiny creatures hidden in the saltwater pools.

When they were teenagers, when their father no longer joined them, Amber would sit with her mother on the headland and watch the surfers paddling out on their bellies, through the white frills of the breakers, then lie in wait on the swells of the sea. One of these was her brother. She loved seeing the skill of the surfboard riders. How they'd pull themselves up to meet the rising waves and ride them to the shore. Her mother watched for sharks. There was a bell you could ring if you sighted one; on the sound, everyone would run from the water. Amber wasn't worried. Her brother was a strong swimmer, like her. How the tide could turn.

That afternoon there was hardly a person between the two headlands that braced the beach like bookends. Perhaps a few fishermen. Amber crossed the shelf of flat black rocks. They were smooth underfoot, mottled with shallow stone bowls filled by the morning tide, like offerings to absent gods. She waded out, letting the waves smash against her and break, until it was deep enough to dive. Then she plunged her body into the abyss of the amniotic sea, pulling herself onward through the soupy water, now swollen with blunt, budding waves. Out and out and out.

She'd drawn herself up where the water was all but still and began to float, her body borne like driftwood on the silvery sea. She closed her eyes against the sun, and felt her eyelids burning, the corners of her eyes stinging with salt. She'd left it too late. It was so far, the sheer distance between them. They'd kept talking on the phone about him coming to visit her in the desert. They'd talked about camping, of going for walks together through the ranges. But it was back. The cancer was back. Seagulls screeched overhead.

Six months later he was in a wheelchair. She'd gone back to Brisbane, back to the island. By then they'd moved his bed downstairs as he could no longer negotiate the ladder which led to the little loft bedroom he'd built for himself and Claire when they renovated the cottage. Windows all sides, it was something like a tower, with enough room only for a double bed. Like something out of a book. A room at the top of a ladder, close to the sky. Up there you could see right over the canopy of trees between the house and the beach, and even glimpse a strip of shimmering turquoise sea. Moving him downstairs placed him in the centre of things, surrounded by the sounds of the domestic, the comings and goings, the hum of the house. But it also signalled an upturning of things, an irreversible shift.

She thinks she has returned many times to those last few weeks of her brother's life, but in truth, when she has felt the memories coming, she has closed the shutters. Tonight, she lets herself re-enter her brother's bedroom. Her mother and she are perched on the edge of the bed. It is a new place for her, to sit at her brother's bedside. She wonders how it is for her mother, to return to the place she would sit when her son was a boy. A place of prayer, of storytelling, of quelling fears borne by the night.

The room downstairs had windows that opened onto a grove of tea-tree that filtered the sun, casting feathery shadows across the bed. Her brother had been asleep for hours that day when he woke, talking. He'd been trying to find a map for her, he said. His speech was slow and laboured. 'I was digging for a map. Then I was digging for cake.'

'What kind of cake?' She incanted the names of cakes their mother used to make, the words releasing tastes trapped under her tongue since childhood. Barmbrack, cinnamon teacake, lemon meringue pie. She recited recipes like nursery rhymes and she saw again lamingtons stacked on cooling racks, walnut loaves nestled in long-tarnished tins, butterfly cakes ready for flight, dusted with icing sugar and filled with fresh cream. Pavlova, caramel slice and chocolate rum pie. On and on she went, crowding the room with cakes, until she remembered she'd actually baked a cake that morning. Something to do with overripe bananas. Something to do.

This is one of the last images she has of her brother. Her brother, who hadn't been able to eat for days, and who had for months been on the strictest of diets, propped up with pillows, making his way slowly through a thick slice of banana cake and a strong milky coffee. Her brother so thin.

His awareness that he was dying came and went. Some days he asked her straight up if he was going to die; other days he talked about getting through this 'hard bit', as if it were a time that might pass. Digging for cake. Searching for treasure, for a turn of the tide, a return ticket back from this certain destination.

It happened that a friend of her parents was leaving the island, and her family saw this as a chance for her to get a lift back to Brisbane. Her mother had already left, planning to return on weekends. Amber took it as a suggestion that it was time for her to go too. That there was no longer room for her. So she said goodbye to her brother, only understanding when it came to the actual point of doing so that she might be saying goodbye forever. Because they didn't know how long – might be days, might be weeks, might even be months.

So she got a lift out of there with strangers, kind strangers, who thankfully didn't pressure her into conversation. They let her sit in the back seat, ticking, as they drove across the lush green island, as they lobbed across the troubled sea, as they drove through interminable traffic to her mother's house, further and further from her brother. Without that map he'd been digging for in his morphine-drenched dreams, she would soon be lost.

She somehow got back to her mother's house. She somehow booked a flight to her faraway home. And she somehow made it back. She needed this, to be home. But she'd not anticipated the distance. Nor that things would happen as they did. For the night after she arrived back, under a full moon, her brother slipped away. *Her brother slipped away.* Her brother – like every human who ever lived, and yet like no one before or after him – departed this world. The idea of a life stopping is implausible, even now, despite the inevitability, the mundanity of it. No matter how low it swoops, it is only when death lands that we know its true weight.

In the Western Desert, references to the dead are avoided. The name a person carried in life is not used for a time, replaced with the word 'kunmanara'. Anyone with the same name or a similar one also becomes kunmanara. For a long time, Amber flinched whenever someone spoke her brother's name. You cannot live side by side with another culture so long and not have it bear upon you. She wanted to leave him rest. Leave him rest in the deeper soils of herself. Don't dig him up.

For over a year she has been treading water, unable to keep still. To be still makes her vulnerable to these memories that filter from the past, that burn through her like photographic images. If she lets them form completely, she feels the breath pressed out of her. But if she shuts them out, she risks the absolute loss of him.

She thinks of the sailor, alone at sea, longing for his daughter. Did he dwell so long on the face of his beloved child that he kept her from death, and from life? In her tiredness, Amber's thoughts become tangled, untrusted. *Am I he?* Or is it foolish to think that grief could draw her brother back to the surface? Is it herself she has abandoned to the open sea?

PLACE BECOMES SPACE AGAIN

The next morning Amber drives east, to the neighbouring community where she will fuel up before she leaves. Despite her lack of sleep, she is wide awake, ready for the long drive home. She's impatient to get moving. People have set up a makeshift camp of tents and wiltjas, or *shelters*, behind the store. Other families from the empty community have been absorbed into households here. Most people are kin, but the whole community is brushed by the death. They will wait here until the funeral is finished. 'Ngaltutjara,' they say again and again as she shakes the hands of the young man's family. *Poor thing.*

Outside the store, a line of kids loops relentlessly around the railing, gangly legs shooting off at all angles. Along the wall a few men gather. When Amber moves to leave, a young woman approaches. Amber recognises her, though her hair has been cut short. She had taken part in a school holiday program Amber had worked on several years ago. They'd been making films. This young woman wanted to tell her story. She had been a petrol sniffer at the age of twelve or thirteen but had recovered.

'He was my brother,' she says, catching Amber off guard.

Amber reaches out a hand. As they touch, she feels a surge of sadness. She swallows. She cannot speak.

'You got that photo?' The young woman reminds her about a photograph she'd taken, of a group of young men outside the store. They'd been playing football on the oval, and when they'd seen the youth workers taking photos with the kids, they'd posed against the wall, arms around one another's shoulders.

The young woman crouches beside Amber and marks each man with a stroke in the dust. 'Nyangatja,' she tells her. *This one*. She traces one stroke over and over with the tip of her finger to show her brother's place in the line. Whether it is the moment or the photograph she is remembering Amber cannot be sure. But the image is fixed in her mind.

Traditionally, images of the dead are avoided in this country. Even if photos are kept, they are stashed away for only particular people to see. But more and more people are asking to see photos, especially young people who have grown up with them.

After years of living in the desert, images of the dead disturb Amber too. They confuse what is reachable and what is not. When her brother passed away, her mother sent photos of him which she had to put away. She could not look at them. Amber promises she will go through the photos when she gets back to town and find this one.

'For family,' the young woman explains.

Amber drives out past the makeshift memorial and towards the turnoff. 'Little memories' was what someone once called these roadside memorials. Already the wind has strewn the flowers across the road, scattering stems and plastic petals into a carpet of colour on the red dirt. 'From dust you are created and unto dust you shall return' – this is what Amber was told as a child. When her brother died, his body wasn't buried. He'd asked to be cremated, that his ashes be buried in the backyard of the house he'd built by the sea.

She imagines the dead as spirits travelling on the wind to find the pastures of their repose. She hasn't prayed for years, but finds herself praying that the young man finds rest. Already his family have emptied the house where he lived and burnt or thrown away his belongings. It was explained to her that when someone passes away here, their house or camp is cleared out, their name erased. In a sense, their place is returned to space again. Returned to dust. Place becomes space again.

LANDSCAPES LOST AND FOUND

A solitary wedge-tailed eagle ruffles the stillness of the morning sky as Amber heads home. The first time she saw these magnificent birds she was travelling up the highway on her way to the desert. It is sobering to watch them tear carcasses apart on the tar with their talons, like ancient gods.

The wedge-tail surfs the thermal currents on upswept wings. Down it soars, wings slicing the sky, just ahead of the moving vehicle. Close enough to see the splayed tail, diamond-shaped, the feathered feet, the sheer mass of brown bird whose outstretched wings might span two metres.

No matter how far they fly, birds are able to return to their nest sites, guided by stored information or memory of the landscapes of their lives. In times of cold or drought or catastrophe – when they are forced to move miles away – they rely upon remembered cues for their return, to tell them they are in the right country. Some birds return to the same nest sites their whole lives.

Do we have these in us, these cues for country? And if we do, how far back do they stretch? She thinks of her ancestors, from Ireland and Scotland and Wales, crossing endless seas to journey to this continent one hundred and fifty years ago. What did they carry of the cues for their homelands, and what became of these? Green hills, silver skies, dark, damp, mossy woods, like picture books clutched to their hearts. Opened like pages to the Australian sun, blasted by relentless light, surely they faded in time?

After they came to the city when she was a child, she'd carried the country they'd left, large and luminous inside her, for many years. She felt, for a long time, a sense of being 'more country than city'. It was an identity constantly affirmed by her mother, who always introduced the family as 'from the country'. She once told Amber with a certain measure of pride how someone had observed how her children always looked to the ground when walking. 'Country kids,' she'd nodded proudly. 'Always on the lookout for snakes.'

It came as a shock at a certain age to realise she'd lived more of her life in the city than in the country. That those early years were to be apportioned an increasingly smaller margin in the timeline of her life. It was an identity that seemed to lack legitimacy the further she grew away from that place, but one she was afraid to shed. But it dwelt within her, that country – a potent mix of place and people, entwined and inextricable. A dormant site, invisible to the outside eye.

Our loved ones might be landscapes inside us, so intricately woven into the fibres of our being that, from the outside, it may be impossible to see the degree of the undoing. It had been happening for years, when she thinks of it, from the time she was told of the cancer. Stitches dropping inside her, row by row. At the point of his death, she had come completely unravelled, with no idea how to knit herself together again. Like a lost bird, she had circled, trying desperately to land, searching for cues that could guide her home. The cues were there, stored like memories inside her, but her brother was not. It felt like all her memories led to empty places, abandoned sites where something had once lived.

She had set off like Freyja, the Norse warrior goddess, who refused to accept her beloved's death. So she had begun, with outstretched falcon's wings, to search the earth for him. She needed to return to the place she grew up, though she didn't know what she would find there. It was an instinctual decision, but once the idea had been conceived, Amber felt compelled to go. Her mother said she would come.

It was only as they approached the small country town that Amber realised she was about to undo a clutch of memories that had been resting, undisturbed, since she was six years old. They swooped back into it, the place her mother had wanted to stay. She was now the age of her mother when she'd left. With two kids. Amber tried to imagine two kids bundled up for leaving.

They swept through the town that first afternoon, without stopping. Straight through the main street, where the shops had shut for the day. The place seemed abandoned. Like a table laid and waiting for the guests to arrive; cutlery aligned, napkins rolled, waiting to be undone. They would come back later to stay at one of the hotels, but first they followed the main road out towards the cattle station.

They passed the school. Little school on stilts with a red iron roof. The first school. Bottle trees along the fence and a weeping willow shadowing the site where the swings used to sweep the air. Steel sinks in the basement, where they'd lather their arms in soapy water up to the elbows before lunch. The lady on the stairs with a rifle. Somebody's mother, convinced the teacher had been picking on her son. School assembly outside in the heat, the national anthem blaring from the verandah.

They crossed the creek and headed down the dirt road that once used to carry them home. Amber was relieved that the road remained unsealed. She imagined the tracks of the old Valiant deep beneath the road's skin, the palimpsest of past journeys in the coming home car. They rattled down Little

Creek Road and towards the house. The memory in place. The house in place. The place of daydreams. What would she become? She remembered herself as much as she remembered the things that happened here. The first house. The felt house. The first map to claim her.

'Green Acres' was cast in cursive across the rusted gates, which no longer met but were wrenched together with wire, unwillingly. Where they used to wait for the school bus, her and her brother and the neighbours' kids, all lined up along the iron gates, like clothes pegs on a washing line. The clarity of the memory is photographic. Yet nothing to reference the small bodies that once sat along those gates. No sign, nor scar, nor evidence. No brother.

'Green Acres'. The name had always struck her as cruelly ironic, never fitting with the world of drought in which she grew up. But the country was green when they went back, and her mother said it was like this when they'd bought the property in the early seventies. Still, the cleared farming land seemed stark after Amber's time living in wilder landscapes. She asked her mother what she knew of the original owners of the land, but her mother mistook the question as being about the people they'd purchased the property from. Amber pushed a little but her mother didn't know. How quickly the past can be covered over, and how incurious those who come after.

The shed. The house. The bougainvillea. The isolated place. Stories of people who filtered in and out of their small world, her mother told her. Names were spoken like incantations of a lost or secret language, wrenching memories from a place that, until now, lived only inside her. Roger. Geoff. Ian and Ted. 'You remember Mrs Thompson?' As her mother spoke, not pictures but feelings came that Amber couldn't keep hold of. Like the smell of the creeks. Might have been water and moss and lantana all mixed up, but she'd never smelt it since, not anywhere else, and when it came it was like it could put her back together, could compress all that'd happened and all that'd been into one moment.

She didn't remember Mrs Thompson as a person or a face. She remembered crawling in and out of rusted car bodies dumped at the front of their neighbour's house. Biscuits and tea on the verandah. Sweet things. A squinted eye. A stale smell.

The man in the driver's seat might have been fifty-something. He was still good-looking. Amber knew him straightaway, though it'd been nearly thirty years. The neighbour's son. Geoff Thompson. He'd bought their house. He'd bought half the district and handed his mother's house down to his son. He still looked after his brother. 'You must have been one of the little ones,' he'd said to Amber.

Don't say his name, Amber prayed. *Don't ask about him.*

Yes, Amber was one of the little ones who lived on the neighbouring property. Scratching round, eyes to the ground, like chooks. The mother keeping them together. The mother who had wanted to stay. To keep them safe in the house. The house their father had built.

So that was the house. White paint, green iron roof, back verandah with a ramp leading down to the lemon trees. There was the shed where the snake had once coiled under the roof. Where she'd sculpted mud shoes with her brother and baked them in the sun. They'd measured how far they could walk before the clay cracked. There was the track to the windmill where she'd walked with her mother to take 'smoko' to her dad in the wide-open days before school. And beyond that, near the hill, the cave where she never went but which her brother said was full of moths, so she filled it with more moths than he could think about and trapped that picture in her head. All the things you keep in your head. The wanted and the unwanted.

The house. The shed. The shouting. The stillness after of a family in bed.

Geckos clicked along the ceiling. Music boxes tinkled. A ballerina on a spring. Fans ploughed the summer air. Heat outside and in. Children breathed the dry night air. Dreamed themselves forwards and backwards in time. Mozzie nets and snakes. Even in the bedroom, snakes. Even under the bed.

That was the world her father built. The things she would keep in her head. The house. The shed. Magenta flowers. Inside the house was a walk-in pantry with a sliding door. Inside the pantry, at the end of the shelf, was a strip, like a ladder, of lead pencil rules, with names and dates printed neatly along each of them. Her father's writing, capital letters, marking the measure of her brother and her with every passing year. Etching their names into the world. Her brother's pencil line always a few inches above hers, out of reach. Even when she stretched her spine til she thought she would snap. The wooden ruler balanced on her head, her back pressed against the pantry wall. The ruled line. The unruly kids. Perhaps their names had been painted over. Or scrubbed clean. Perhaps they'd been overlooked.

Amber longed to get inside and see for herself. To excavate the site, to find the record of them. To unearth the cattle bones beneath the floorboards, or sit on the bench between the lemon trees and listen for his voice. But they weren't invited in. After a pleasant exchange with her mother, Geoff continued on his way. And they were left, outside the house her father had built, without legitimate claim.

At the hotel that night, they picked through the family bones again. There was still some meat on them. Her mother told the story of how her father had thrown her brother into the river to teach him how to swim. 'He was *drowning*,' she said. The cruelty of men. Her father's impatience for his son to be a man. To show how it was done. Her mother's shoulders crumbled like her body could no longer contain these memories. Of the times she might have saved her son. It's not like they hadn't been here before but there were always more details that might help make sense of things. They both needed to make sense of things.

When her mother left her father all those years later, it was not apparent to him why. There was no single incident, no fight, no infidelity. There must have been something that tipped things over, of course. But it may have been the smallest wind, an outgoing tide, a cool change. Whatever it was it carried with it a litany of events, of disappointments, of betrayals, that reached right back to this place, where they first came after their marriage, where the children were born and where she became a mother and soon found herself quite alone. When he'd come in in the evenings, she was brimming with stories of her children's little antics and developments, but he would brush past her, saying he needed a shower. After his shower he didn't ask, and she didn't tell. It seemed inconsequential, the world of a wife. He'd sit on the verandah sipping beer while she cooked and fed the kids ahead of them. At the dinner table, he talked about his day and she listened. And later, after she put the children to bed, there seemed no relief from the isolation of a day.

They walked under lemony streetlights that evening, orbited by insects, while her mother narrated a map which once had function and meaning. The old town was only a few streets. The main street stretched like a spine down the middle, with an island of garden beds where roses once grew. The man in that shop (what did he do?) who used to tease her with her stuffed bear called Beary. 'Hairy!' he would say, and her mother would turn inwards with a forced laugh to reassure her it was to be taken in jest. A man who made cordial. She remembered them taking the bottles back for refills. What did she really remember? The clanking of empty glass in wooden crates. The smell of the colour red.

On the main street there was now a museum. They picked up a brochure that said the town had originally been developed as a service centre for the short-lived gold rush towns nearby. The mine featured in all of the pamphlets. Operating since 1888, it was cited as 'an extraordinary example of how humans can literally convert a mountain into a hole'. It was an extraordinary statement, almost vulgar in its triumphant tone, its shameless celebration of ruin. Amber felt a groundswell of anger and grief inside her. It made her aware of how she'd come to see country. Not only was her grief for the land itself, but for the stories she knew were held within its folds.

In the desert, the stories for the country seeped through, so that even if you never heard the full story, you would soon hear references to totemic ancestors and their travels, intricately bound to the country, and believed to be still exerting influence on the present. In town where she lived, sometimes you stumbled across plaques that granted some small opening, like a portal into the past, so that soon land became almost an animate thing to her, more than the sum of its physical or apparent parts. When she started to know Aboriginal people she started to hear more, and it was like flesh was returned to the bones of the land. Even if she couldn't remember the names of all the places she learned about, or the details of the narrative, the country had expanded irrevocably for her, called to the surface of the sea of conscious thought.

Once she started to see like this, it was impossible to unsee. Then impossible not to apply this seeing to everywhere. *Terra nullius*, she came to feel, not only denied sovereignty to the land's Aboriginal custodians, but conveyed a sense of nothingness or absence, blind to the stories inscribed within it, and the knowledge bound up in them. She had come to think of country as particular. Not as space, but place, to someone. And this made her want to know about other places too. She remembered being told as a child that both the name of the town and the name of her first school were 'Aboriginal' names, though no explanations of their meanings or derivations were given. The school name, she heard, was a word for 'sharp' or 'upright stones'. But to whom, and when?

She often wondered if her longing for home was rooted here, in this childhood place, but what did she hope to find here? She knew it was romantic to imagine she belonged in an isolated country town. Who would she have been, had she stayed? Perhaps the longing she'd lived with was simply the weight of the traveller's luggage, a weight that might never shift.

Before they left, Amber and her mother drove past the old house again. One last look before leaving – maybe they'd even drop in. Like pulling old clothes from the cupboard just for one last try. But there was no one around. They chose to let it be, to fold the past and shelve it once again. The house in place. But the memories undone and spilling.

Away sweeps a sea of pastel green, both sides of the moving vehicle. The road so straight, so constant, so clear. Ahead, the distant watercolours deepen as she approaches, the details clarify. Far away, vertical shafts of rain. Behind her, she imagines the country quietly vanishing, sealing over as she passes, like the floating village that only appears with the tug of someone's longing. She has longed for this country, dreamt of it, returned by remembered cues. Already she feels the ache of leaving, not knowing when she'll be back. In coming and going she has created a kind of schism within herself. She can never truly belong in the desert, in the way the people here do, but nor can she belong any place else.

Then again, is place only a part of it? Is this the reason she returned? She thinks of Andrew. She thinks of her brother. The landscapes inside us can never truly be lost. Maybe we can only belong to each other.

She thinks about Andrew's desire to be buried in the country he's come to call home. She will find out what she can, and help him to have the funeral he wants. It is something she can do for her friend. The thought brings a small, unexpected glint of excitement. It's only been four days but she feels she's been gone too long. She will drive all day, and into the night, to get back.

WILTJA, SHELTER FROM THE WIND

Outside, a westerly sweeps in broad, unbridled strokes across the sparsely treed country. No windbreaks. Willy-willies skim the surface of the land, once right on the road in front of the car. But even so the country seems still, as if nothing can ruffle it. It is only when she stops for a break that she feels the force of it. As she climbs from the car, the Toyota door swings back and slams against her body. She feels light, like she might be swept up in its dance, her hair in disarray. She remembers Jennifer's stories about people being blown from their beds, and smiles at the image.

A few metres off the road, a rusted-out car lies tipped on its bonnet. She wanders over, her body a buffer to the wind. Closer, she sees that wild grasses grow through the upturned carcass; pale purple wildflowers push through the defunct chassis. She walks around and squats behind the shell. It is so still. She presses her spine against the steel. Behind her, the car body feels like a huge and gentle beast, breathing close.

The car is my shelter, she thinks. A bulwark against the elements. A temporary windbreak, a wiltja. There is no sound but the noise of the wind, lashing madly through the papery grass, tunnelling through the car skeleton, whirring around like a spirit. A line comes to her from a book a friend gave her last year: 'Let the wind blow through you.' Her friend was Buddhist, and here were the words of her teacher. When she handed it to her, Amber saw the hope in her friend's eyes, how dearly she'd wanted to help. Amber also hoped for this, the teaching that might turn things around. But she couldn't take it in. She had no room, no matter how hungry she was. But it seems these words have slipped through the hairline cracks after all. *Let the wind blow through me, let it clear me out.*

Maybe it was something she knew all along. That the elements could speak to you, that nature could leave signs. She used to call it God, whatever it was. But this is because this presence was named before she could name it for herself. It took her a long time to un-name it. To just let it be what it was. How the wind would come up, a bird could come to you. How a pair of bats would suddenly scatter from the banana trees at the bottom of the garden. They were signs she didn't need to decode or convert into words. They let her know she wasn't alone. She was part of the play of things. But when she lost her brother, she lost sight of these things. It was as if the world no longer spoke to her. And this made her feel unbearably alone.

For a few moments she stays crouched behind her wiltja, savouring the small pause before the journey home. It is only when she makes to leave that she notices a nest, woven with grass and mud, up in an empty cavity where a wheel once was. The clay is a similar copper colour to the oxidised paintwork so that at first the nest is camouflaged. Closer, she sees how a single strand of red cotton has been intricately threaded through the weave. So exquisite the artistry of earth and grass, fashioned by the beak of a wild bird.

When she was a child, there were always wasps' nests by the water tank. And the tightly woven, cup-like homes of willie wagtails, covered with the thin membrane of spider's web and lined with grass, sometimes animal hair. Her brother warned her never to touch a nest or the birds would abandon it. So she leaves it as she finds it and walks towards the car. But as she does, she hears her brother's voice: 'Look what a bird has left you!' She takes it as a gift, this tiny nest, from her brother, from the country itself. *So the world is offering things again.*

Coming home

Darkness blackens the space between things, blunts the visible, so that, as Amber drives into town, her eyes are apportioned small scenes at a time. Vignettes of a place that can be no other. It makes the transition between worlds less brutal. The highway is a kind of liminal strip that links the outlying lands with what has become an urban townscape. Intermittent buildings, unlit; a belt of windows set back from the road, like little suspended squares of buttery light, tells her she is passing the outlying town camps. Suddenly everything presses close – the ranges, the trees, the hills. She has left the wide-open spaces.

She feels an ample shift as the car comes through the gap and continues to drop speed. The noise of the engine encroaches, the churning sound of the tyres is increasingly present. It is as if she has been hurtling forward in the body of an unstoppable beast for hours. Now it is as if the animal has been wounded and is crawling home.

As the car skirts the roundabout and follows the sandy river, Amber feels a gear shift inside herself. Now needing to concentrate on road rules and traffic and navigation. To watch for people. It is always like this, coming back. The conscious need to gather oneself in from one's roamings, to rein in the mind. She feels both resistance and relief. She has been a long way away.

At home, there is no one. The flat is empty and Ruth is still away. Nothing but the boxes she'd started to bring in from the shed the night she got back. When she goes to light the stove, she finds the gas is out. She curses because it's cold and she can't use the heater. And because she wants a cup of tea. She'd forgotten the state of the flat, not yet ready for habitation. She thinks to go outside and make a fire but she's too tired. She unrolls the swag in the middle of the lounge room, peels back the khaki canvas and crawls inside. Red sand spills on the grey slate, fine as sifted flour.

She wakes in the night from the deepest sleep, hungry. She crawls out of the swag and goes to the fridge. The light spills across the floor, and reveals the old suitcase. She grabs the leftover sandwich she bought at the roadhouse along the way and walks over to open the case. She draws out her brother's artworks, half-bound in strips of bubble wrap.

There are two pieces, both pen and ink. One is the rough side of a cliff reaching up from a river, with houses that appear to be growing out of the top of it. The way he has drawn it, the houses become another stratum of sediment in a landscape composed of lines. The other is a portrait, which Amber has always imagined to be a self-portrait, though this might not actually be right. In any case, it is the outline of a person, and it too is filled with sediment – like layers of country. Amber has looked at this pair of artworks so many times but still they seem to offer more.

Now she notices something she's not paid much attention to before. Her brother's name is signed in the bottom right corner of each piece. Like an epitaph. Here and gone at once, her brother. Like their names on the pantry wall in the house in the country. For the first time it doesn't distress her. Tonight, his presence is a pulse, strong and fierce and unbroken, even by death. Amber looks around the room. The picture hooks are still on the walls. She takes her brother's artworks and hangs them, side by side.

HOW SHALL WE BURY HIM?

In the morning she makes a fire outside and boils the billy for a cup of tea. Then she is ready to unpack the car and sort out the gas. All her efforts feel like preparation for going to see Andrew, getting herself ready. Is she ready? How can she ever be ready to watch a friend die? When she saw him only a few days ago she was already bracing against grief. She felt she couldn't handle another death, couldn't lose another part of her. But she is no longer running. She will be with him till the end, and after that as well. Of course she wants to hold his hand and stop him from going forward. To slow things down. But she knows that to reduce his life into these last few weeks is to deny the life that's been. She can't be with him every day, but she can do what he's asked of her. She can help him create something beautiful to send him off.

She opens her computer and begins to read about what is possible for burial. As she thought, in this part of the country at least, bodies can only be buried in a cemetery or on private property. But there are options other than timber coffins as a way to go into the ground. She reads about people sewing shrouds to wrap their loved ones in. About cardboard coffins that disintegrate faster than wood.

Her research takes her to the burial practices of the Anglo-Saxons. She reads about funerary pyres, and how they used to burn the personal effects of the dead. In other cases, grave goods were placed with the body in the earth, like a final and enduring portrait of the deceased. She finds herself reading about grave markers, like stones and wooden stakes, and the burial mounds of the Anglo-Saxon landscape, where death was ever-present in a world of war and fate. Until she realises she has gone way off track. She is putting off going to see him. What of the funeral? She has no idea what he actually wants.

The next morning she goes to Andrew's house. His mother answers the door. She says he is still sleeping, but invites her in to wait. Amber follows her through the quiet house to the kitchen. While Lyn makes her a cup of tea, she tells Amber he has taken a turn for the worse. 'I just wonder,' she says, 'if it's not time?' His mother's eyes tear up.

Amber thinks of her own mother, her sister-in-law, the aloneness of the carer. She steps forward to touch her arm but Lyn quickly shakes it off. 'Sorry,' she says, as if pulling in a part of herself that is about to escape. 'I'm just a bit tired today.'

Time to take him to hospital – is that what she means? But before Amber can check, the kettle boils. His mother darts to it like a bird to prey, pours the boiling water into a ceramic Japanese teapot and places it on the kitchen bench between them. She brings two small matching cups, with no handles, the colour of green stone. *The place of beauty*, thinks Amber, *in balancing the darkness*. 'Milk and sugar?' Then they both turn to the sound of Andrew coughing. 'I'll get him a cup. I'm sure he'll have tea.' Lyn goes ahead of Amber with a hot cup of tea. At the bedroom door she announces that Amber is here.

'Hello,' he says wearily, but he is clearly pleased to see her. He does look worse. His skin seems thin. His eyes dark. He is having trouble breathing. He's not sitting up but is slumped into a stack of pillows, like a puppet, strings relaxed.

'Like anything to eat?' says his mother. 'A sandwich? Piece of toast? Or some soup? I made some pumpkin soup last night. Might be easier to swallow?'

He shakes his head. 'I'm right for now, thanks, Mum. The tea's good.'

'Then I'll leave you two to it,' she says, hurrying to the door.

'Feel free to stay,' Amber starts, but she is already in flight, and quickly gone.

'You're back early?' he says.

'I know. It didn't work out. Stuff happening in the community.'

'Really?'

She is avoiding mentioning the death of the young man. It doesn't feel right to be talking about it.

'But it was good. I mean, good things happened.'

'For example?' He smiles.

She thinks for a minute. So many things, but hard to explain. She fears they may amount to nothing if spoken. It's all a bit of a dream, now she's back. A floating village far at sea.

'I found a nest on the way home,' she says. 'This most intricately woven nest, made of mud and grass. It was inside this rusted-out car on the side of the road. It even had a strand of red cotton woven into it. I thought of you.'

Was that right? Had she thought of Andrew? It was actually her brother she had thought of, at the time. But she might have thought of Andrew too. The nest seemed to weave the two men together.

She pulls her laptop out of her bag. 'So, I've been doing some reading, this morning, about burials.'

Andrew's eyes light up. 'We're going to have a funeral pyre on top of a hill?'

She smiles. 'Funnily enough, I did read about funerary pyres, but I'm afraid you can't have one in this country. Not unless you want your family to go to prison.'

He sighs. 'Ah well.'

'And neither can you be left to the eagles and dingoes, so don't even ask.'

'So you're saying I can't be sent out to sea on a flaming ship?'

'I thought you wanted to be buried in the desert?'

Andrew laughs, then starts to cough. He reaches for the tea.

'It's cemetery or private land,' she continues, 'unless you're cremated. Then we can scatter you anywhere.'

'You know,' he says when he's finished coughing, 'I know what I said, but I'm actually quite keen on the cemetery. It'll make me feel a part of the town, its history. I just want to go straight back to the earth, like my dog – no barriers.'

'Sounds like that's not allowed. But you can have a cardboard coffin if you want.' She reads from the screen. 'Or wicker, or seagrass, or apparently felted wool. These coffins will break down a lot sooner than oak.'

'Cardboard, please! Then we can paint it. So if we go to the cemetery first, maybe we can go on somewhere afterwards? Somewhere, you know, in nature.'

'*We*?'

'I mean *you*, yes,' he laughs. 'You can drop me in the ground at the cemetery, then you can all go off somewhere together and have a nice time.'

He starts to cough again, a dry, rasping cough, and all at once the lightness in the conversation is snuffed out. She passes him a glass of water. It will not be a nice time. It will be a time without him. She feels her body tighten.

'You could have a feast,' he says between coughs. 'Or a massive funerary pyre.'

The pyre again. 'And burn what?'

His mother appears at the door with a glass of water and a strip of tablets. She moves to her son, punching out pills from the tinfoil and placing them in his open hand.

Amber gets up from the bed. 'I'll go,' she says. 'Best that you rest.'

'Thank you,' he says, managing an apologetic smile.

'I'll keep thinking,' she says.

His mother moves into Amber's imprint on the bed.

As she passes through the lounge, a strange assemblage of small, amorphous figures catches her eye. They are arranged in rows, like a toy army, on a timber table under the window. She approaches them. He'd only started on these around the time she left. And here they are, a whole tribe of them.

Carefully, she picks up one of the small figures. It fits in her hand like a fresh egg, with a little more weight perhaps, but equal warmth. The polished timber is smooth against her skin and the beauty of the wood inherent, in the way of trees and seeds and pods. But the subtle work of the sculptor has made it something else, something familiar, if impossible to reach. Something primordial, instinctive. It's like holding a live creature in her hand – an injured bird perhaps, on account of its stillness. She places it back amongst its kin, feeling the print of its departure in her palm.

CEREMONY

Before her next visit, Amber returns to her research on funerary pyres. Descriptions of bodies reduced to smoke and ash laid upon pyres sound gruesome, but what captures her imagination is the spectacle of it – the physicality of the wood, the roaring flames, the burning pile of the deceased one's personal effects. It made for certain memorialisation.

'You could always have a pyre of something else,' she says when she goes to see Andrew. 'If you're still attached to the idea.'

'We could burn all my things!' he says.

'No!' she cries.

'Why not?' he says. 'It's all natural – the artworks, anyway.'

Amber is horrified. She tells him about her brother's artworks and how they hold his presence alive for her.

'But you've got to let go—' he starts.

'I will never let go of him.'

There is nothing more to say. Tears come for both of them.

'Sorry,' she says, wiping her eyes.

'Oh, don't apologise,' he says, tears running down his face. And though each of them tries to speak, to console the other, the words crumble in their mouths, until they are both laughing and crying at once.

'Okay,' says Andrew, composing himself. 'How about wood? Can everyone bring wood?'

Amber smiles through her tears, reaching for a tissue. 'We can all bring wood,' she says. 'How about a pyre of burning wood? Or anything else people want to burn?'

'Okay – as long as it's natural. We don't want any of those nasty incinerations like we had when we were kids.'

'If you want to let go of your things, how about a separate installation that people can take something from to remember you?'

In this way the two of them dream up a sort of ceremony that Andrew wants to take place in a riverbed, in a gap in the ranges just out of town. They'll need to get permission first, but there have been weddings and parties there over the years. He wants the ceremony to happen after the cemetery. And for as long as he stays awake that day, she asks him about readings and songs and pieces of music he'd like to be played. She helps him remember his friends. And when she goes home, she writes it all down, like a story to read back to him.

THE ABSENCE OF LANDMARKS AND BEARINGS

Weeks pass like this. Meanwhile, Amber hears news that Jennifer's mother, Lena, has been flown to town and admitted to hospital. Another stroke. They say it's unlikely she will recover, this time. The succession of sad news seems unbearable but it makes Amber think. You cannot extract sorrow from life. It is also part of the play of things.

Out the front of the hospital, people congregate on a small wedge of lawn that functions something like a town square. Mostly Aboriginal patients and their families – some from town, some in from outlying communities. Cars cruise by, slow down as they pass. People lean out of windows, call out, see who's here. One old man lies on his side on a narrow steel bed they've wheeled out to park in the sun, drip still attached and pumping. Another sits, stooped, on a plastic chair by his side. They trade a cigarette between them. People come and go all day, the various configurations like a kaleidoscope turning with the hours. When Amber arrives on her bike she has a flash of a chorus of angels, all in white and pale green hospital gowns, sitting under a sky that's bruised and bearing down. Might be rain.

All along the ward, through open doors old men and women are lying, televisions blaring. On the floor above, a different scene entirely. The maternity ward is where she'd spent most time at this hospital, visiting young women with their new babies who she'd worked with in town and out bush. It was always a bustling place, full of families and children, young women and men, eyes sparkling. Most of these new mothers were very young. Many of them teenagers. Many without the support of the father. But no matter the circumstances of each of them, Amber saw how having a baby singled people out, elevated them. Giving birth placed them at the centre, surrounded by everyone's joy and affection, even if only for a brief while. Any concerns she had about their ability to manage, or about them being consumed by motherhood, with the loss of their own aspirations or freedom, were eclipsed in the halcyon days after birth.

But this ward has a different tone. Lena is propped up on a pile of pillows and stiff white sheets when Amber edges through the partially open door. A nurse empties a plastic eggcup of drugs into her hand then leaves, barely acknowledging her. 'Kapi?' Lena asks pitifully, in place of a greeting. She has not been left any water. Her face is collapsed on one side, her speech is slurred. She shows Amber that she can't move her arm or leg, on the left side. She tries to reach with her right arm across to the dinner that has been placed on a mobile table on her left. Amber wheels the table around to her good side and looks for something to wipe the side of her food-smeared face. As Lena eats, a portion of each spoonful misses and spills onto her nightgown.

Behind a thin green curtain, a woman from a neighbouring community is sleeping. She sleeps for the entire time Amber is here. Her snoring is surprisingly comforting. Lena is lucky to have someone she knows sharing the room. It can often be a stranger, with their strange visitors. Amber thinks of the faraway places these ladies have come from. Communities humming with car engines and country and western music, the incessant comings and goings and gatherings of kids, families, camp dogs and cars; the scent of charred meat and open fires. Big skies bearing down. The unending band of horizon. As she wipes the old lady's face, she thinks of Lena all those years ago, out in a valley laden with mingkulpa that coloured the country purple for a time. 'This is my ngura,' she had pronounced, standing straight amidst a group of women, bent and picking. Then, sweeping an arm along the length of the ranges, as if to underline them, she'd repeated, 'This is my country.'

Where is that country from here? Can she reach it at night when she closes her eyes? Above the stench of disinfectant and the sound of the television blasting? Through the touch of stale white sheets and pale green plastic everything? In the absence of landmarks and bearings, can she follow her cues for country?

When the time came, her brother wouldn't go to hospital. He wanted to stay in his house, with his family around him. And now Andrew, who knows it's considered selfish to burden his family and friends with his care. But after years of making a home, surely your house should hold you in the end? Her brother had apologised when his condition got worse and he could no longer walk. He needed help to go to the toilet, to leave the bedroom. He felt humiliated by this dependency. But for her sister-in-law, for all of them, it was a chance to share something of the load he'd been burdened with. Something they could do for him.

Soon Lena's eyes become heavy and talking becomes a strain. Maybe Amber can bring her some mingkulpa in the morning, if she can find some around town. As she goes to leave, the old lady gestures to the television mounted on the ceiling between the beds, and indicates that she wants the channel changed. Amber finds the remote control on the bedside table and flicks through the programs, waiting for approval. Lena chooses a game show. When Amber passes her the control, she turns up the volume so that all at once the room is ringing with bells and buzzers and raucous clapping.

'Are you sure you want this one?' Amber checks.

'Uwa,' she says. 'For company.'

Outside, the sky has fallen. Rain pounds the pavement as if some kind of sky god is stamping out the sadness of the day. A couple of patients shelter under a small overhang near the hospital entrance. Pressed against the glass wall, they watch the downpour. Amber rides her bike along the main road, then takes a back street to meet the track that follows the river home. She is already drenched by the time she gets this far, but she couldn't wait to get out of there.

As she rides through sheets of rain, she thinks of that old woman up there on the third floor, with a television for company and a husband so far away. The little nest where they'd lived, the puppies, the people who they belonged to, who belonged to them. She thinks of Lena's place in the world, that vast expanse of country, no parts unknown to her. How her life has been knitted into that country from birth. Even before. How cruel it seems, at the end of the road, to be uprooted.

What Amber doesn't know as she rides through the rain is that, somewhere out there, Jennifer is on her way, on the road. If she drives all day she will make it by nightfall. She has Alfie with her, her two youngest children, her sister. And Shyanna has convinced her mother to bring just one puppy for her grandmother. As the car rides the corrugations of the dirt road, the puppy nuzzles its soft head into the crook of the little girl's arm. Shyanna sinks into her sister's shoulder and soon they are both asleep.

Benevolent Spirit

Amber is pleased to see Jennifer's face through the window later that night. When she opens the door, Shyanna crouches at the doorway and opens her arms, spilling the puppy onto the slate floor. It runs about, sniffing at Amber's things, then promptly lifts a hind leg and squirts urine on the rug. 'Ai!' Jennifer growls, and both Shyanna and, behind her, Brianna run to grab the puppy, ashamed. But Amber's laughter reassures them and their gasps turn to giggles. It lifts the mood of all of them. They make a fire outside and cook chops. They don't talk much about Lena. They don't talk much, really. They mostly sit and watch the flames creep around the caverns of burning wood.

Jennifer gets up early to go to the hospital. Shyanna is upset: her mother won't let her take the puppy. After tantrums and tears it is resolved, and Amber is left with this little tiger striped pup, who bounces about the flat all morning. She can't put it outside for fear it will slip through the fence and onto the road. She must keep it with her.

For a while after they leave, it scratches at the timber door, crying for Shyanna, so Amber calls it over and tries to hold it while she continues to work at her desk. But the dog keeps reaching its snout forwards and trying to chew at the computer cable, forcing her to put it down again. As soon as its paws hit the floor it finds the hanging cord and starts to gnaw again, until Amber is forced to leave her desk and sit with her laptop in the middle of the bed, like an island. Immediately the puppy leaps onto the bed and starts to pull at the blanket with its tiny sharp teeth. Amber holds one hand on its belly, attempting to calm it, but it only coils around her arm, finding the game in all her actions.

This goes on for a while, until the puppy rolls over, gets up and goes for the computer cable again. Exasperated, Amber puts the computer aside and hauls the writhing animal into her lap. Cradled in the cross of her legs, it is suddenly calm. In moments, it closes its eyes and sinks the warm shape of itself into the hollow. Unable now to reach the laptop with both hands, Amber sighs, and nurses the sleeping puppy. A benevolent little spirit, in the guise of chaos, has come to stir up the gravity of the situation. This gives Amber an idea.

When she arrives at Andrew's house, there are other friends leaving. They say he's been falling in and out of sleep. Amber pokes her head around the door with the puppy, whose whimpering gives their presence away immediately.

'What have you got there?' Andrew asks. As she enters the room, he grins. 'Bring it here, bring it here!' His words run into each other, as if they've been topped and tailed.

She carries the puppy over and it nuzzles into his neck, sniffing and licking. He laughs. She tries to place it on his lap but it keeps wriggling. She holds its writhing body firm against her chest, and Andrew reaches out a hand to stroke it. From neck to tail he smooths down the puppy's brindle fur until it becomes still, absolutely still. As if it senses his condition.

The week that follows patterns itself like this. Hospital visits. The car pulling up. Family coming and going. But then the family are gone for good, and Amber feels their absence gravely. The little girls especially, as well as the puppy, had brought life to her place. The old lady surprises them all with another recovery, and is declared well enough to go home in a few weeks. 'The old lady lives on!' Jennifer had said when she told Amber the news.

But Andrew does not recover. Death comes more swiftly than they hoped. Maybe it always does. The time she took the puppy to him is the last time she saw Andrew.

The day of his death, she'd been past his house. Spring was coming and though the light was at the window earlier, when she'd passed the house on her morning walk it was too early to visit. When she found out later that he'd died during the night, she kept thinking how strange it was that when she'd walked past the house, he was already gone. That she'd imagined him in there, tucked in his bed. All of a sudden it is a house of things, full and empty at once. She will gather these precious things, these remnants of him, and those the family do not wish to keep she will bring, as he wanted, to the ceremony.

A SKY SO BARE

A string of daytime headlights stretches along the highway as they drive out of town towards the cemetery. Shining as they do, they yet make no imprint on a day already drenched in sunlight. On the car radio Nick Drake croons: 'Saturday sun came early one morning, in a sky so clear and blue . . .' The sky so clear and blue and bare.

A parade of people trails in silence past row after row of neat and tidy tombstones. Mostly slabs of stone or white wooden crosses, they are stark against the faded lawn, relieved by an occasional clasp of colourful plastic flowers made stiff by the sun. There are cities in Europe where the dead are buried up to twelve layers deep for want of space, and the bodies of families laid one atop the other. But in this small town there is pause between graves and space around.

They gather beneath the desert oaks, watch sunlight claw through the sketchy canopy of trees overhead, casting lace-like patterns in the dust. Andrew's death so near that Amber can better imagine him standing tall and graceful, as one of them. Not sealed in a cardboard coffin, painted in native grasses by his fellow artists.

'Saturday sun won't come and see me today . . .'

The service is short, as he had asked. His parents wanted a priest to preside over the ceremony and, after some argument, this wish he granted them. The priest is well chosen. He is young, informal, likeable. He acknowledges the sadness of family and friends but tells them not to lose hope in their grieving. He speaks of this being a celebration of life. Amber winces at this phrase. For her it suggests they should be happy rather than sad. She is not happy. She is mourning. But she knows Andrew saw it like this. He wanted his death to break the gravity of the past year. 'There's been sadness enough,' he said.

In quiet procession, they each place a palm-sized stone upon the ground until a small pyramid of stones is left. A mark of their presence, of his absence. It was what he'd asked for. His artworks had often been installations, often ephemeral, packed up and removed like a tenant's belongings at the end of each exhibition. His motto was to leave no trace. Once he made a series of butterflies, exquisitely crafted from the finest Japanese paper. He painted hundreds of these with watercolours and placed them in various locations around town – on the footbridge that crosses to the east side, on windowsills of shops in the mall, on the lawns near the hospital, outside the courthouse. He left them for people to come upon, or take if they wished. He didn't mind. The idea was an intervention into the mundane world, an interruption. He chose butterflies because they have the shortest lifespan, often living less than two weeks. He said he was doing nothing more than mimicking life. It seems fitting that a tribute to him should soon return to rubble.

Amber places two stones. One for him. One for her brother.

At the end of the ceremony they each throw a handful of red dirt into the grave, with thoughts for the departed. A haze of dust hovers over the ditch. So this is it, the return to dust. The final surrender of our everyday struggles against the encroaching dust. In its finality, the gesture brings a new wave of soundless weeping. Amber casts a handful of dirt into the hole in the ground, where the coffin is still visible. Finally, her friend is returned to the earth.

She walks back through a corridor of graves, stopping to gather a handful of yellow fabric flowers scattered by the wind. She returns them to a small over-tipped jar at the foot of a grave, and adds some dirt to weight it. On most of the headstones the epitaph is brief: name, date of birth, date of death. Is this all that's left of us, she thinks, spare inscriptions on small square plaques, while our bones become sediment in the earth's crust? But here are our names, markers of our individual lives, chronicle of a community passing. They will continue to hold our presence in the world, at least for a time. She hopes Andrew got what he wanted. To be bound to this place by burial, like his dog all those years ago.

But is it only death that binds us so? This is a tender place, she thinks as she leaves the cemetery, a site of sorrow. How many hearts have broken here? What of our sorrow, our joy, our everyday rubbing against the earth where we live out our lives? Maybe all of it, in truth, is what sows us into the soil, making any place some place, and everywhere home.

FIRE IN THE RIVER

Cars pull in along the dry river, all angles in the dirt. When there's no more room, they make a procession across the other side of the road. People stumble down the sandy bank, laden with blankets and swags and baskets and dishes of food. They have all brought something to burn. In the riverbed, a series of tables has been laid out end to end under a magnificent river red gum to create one long setting, dressed in white cotton cloth. Small clutches of wildflowers wade in humble kitchen jars at regular intervals, wine glasses wait to be filled. As people approach, they place their offerings upon the table – food they have made, bottles of wine – so that it slowly becomes a feast.

You might think you had come across a wedding, had you chanced upon this scene in the Saturday sun. But something feels different. Everyone speaks softly, parents hush their children before they send them scattering up the river to play. People embrace, over and over, quiet tears are shed upon each other's shoulders. At the beginning, there is not much more than the sound of car doors shutting, scant conversation. It is a portrait of a community *en plein air*, turned out for a funeral, of a kind.

A few of Andrew's friends take offerings of branches and cut wood and construct a pyre a little way up the creek. It is unusual to make a bonfire here. Here they are used to low-burning, cooking fires, maybe something learned from local people. Little scrapings in the earth's skin, easily sealed over.

It is the clarinet that calls them to attention, that quells any murmuring in the crowd. They look up to where the sound is coming from. There on the rocks, silhouetted against the brilliant blue, is Andrew's friend Matt, his back slightly arched, instrument pointing to the sky. There is a communal, soundless sigh. Maybe it is a single breath, an exhale. Parents squat to point out the source of the sound to their little ones, who, unable to contain their excitement, rush to show another child. Some race towards the rocks, causing a ripple of concern among parents. A few fathers follow in silence and stand at the base of the hill, quietly calling their children back and setting the limit as to how far they can climb.

The music squeezes the sorrow out of everyone. Tears return. Tears for the loss and tears for the beauty, for the breath of the musician, belting out the *Hallelujah* from the hill. *Will grief be ever done?* thinks Amber. But she is thinking something else as well. How futile all our efforts to dodge it, or outrun it, or even to move on from it, as if life was something else, something apart. Some people put an arm around the person next to them, as if to fortify them. Some sit on the pink sand.

As it comes to an end, Amber walks down to the river just a little way to light the pyre. The fire is fast to catch with the load of dry mulga and gum, and soon the community of mourners turn as one, slowly making their way to the burning flames. She watches the crowd come towards her, like a choreography. Like limbs of the same body moving as one. Or is it the river itself coming down? For when the crowd reaches the pyre, it breaks into tributaries that spill either side and surround the fire like a moat.

The fire burns at the centre, magnificent. At first a pyramid of restless flames squabbling for height. They reach for the apex, where the long branches, vertically laid, lean in and touch.

One by one the branches begin to burn until the whole pyre is aflame, a spectacle of dance and brilliant light. It might be a mythical creature, licking and spitting and spiralling towards the sky, now thick with wood smoke. A shapeshifter, at once dead and alive, it is difficult to tell whether its dance is one of ecstasy or pain. Either one is abandonment, a form of madness that meets their grief – unflattened by words, untamed. The mourners remain still all around, but the creature heaves and lurches, unshackled, as if trying to swallow its own body, or fighting life itself.

Everyone stands, looking inwards, transfixed by the blaze. At once a unique assembly, born of this particular death, at once a community around a fire, an age-old tableau, as old as fire itself. Children scuttle backwards and forwards, feeding the creature, pitching twigs and sticks they've fetched, handfuls of papery leaves. Their laugher spills into the silence, uncontainable. For some, this grates. Their parents, sensitive, rein them in. But mostly people smile, grateful for the levity that children bring.

On and on roars the fire, ever upward, until it seems to crescendo, a dazzling pyramid of light. They stand there with nothing to be said. No platitudes, no placations. No words, actually, apart from a whisper now and then. Only the hiss of the resin in the wood, the tunnelling roar of the fire and the weeping. Silent weeping. Some people hold hands, lean into one another, draw their loved ones near. If any bonds have been broken, they are forgiven, if just for tonight.

As the fire quietens, they notice they are also losing daylight. The rock face near the gap glows amber, swathed by the western sun. Some turn to admire it, others turn to one another, uttering words like small bouquets under their breaths. They watch the creature calm down, both relieved and regretful at its passing.

Soon the children begin to tug at their parents, hungry. One by one, people peel away from the fire, and seat themselves on either side of the funeral feast. Candles are lit, drinks are poured, hesitantly at first, as if in fear of being too frivolous. But it was what Andrew wanted. What he asked for. So they have a glass and the food tastes good. And the wine bathes the sting in some of their hearts and lets their insides sway just a little, lets the edges between them slightly blur.

Night ebbs gently in around them. It might be a wedding feast, with the food and the speeches to come. One by one people stand and tell the story lit in their mind when they think of Andrew. An anecdote, a memory, that threads together a lasting narrative of him, and of themselves. But no matter how funny the tale, the teller nearly always cries. Amber wishes she could have done this for her brother.

When it is time to leave, they go by torchlight to the timber table on the other side of the red gum, now resplendent with red silvery lamplight. A fairytale tree, with treasure beneath, for here have been stacked a cairn of Andrew's belongings. Paintings, sculptures, books, souvenirs from his travels. A portrait of him. Grave goods spared from the grave. They each choose something, something to slip into their pocket or hold in their hand. Something to keep of him.

When no one else is there, Amber wanders over to the table and kneels in the sand before it. She knows what she wants. She picks through the leftovers, lit by a small torch, until she sights one of the tiny troupe of strange figures she'd seen on the table in his house, arranged almost like a chessboard. She turns it in her hand, the polished woodgrain smooth against her skin. *Who are you?* Not quite human, but somehow suggestive of human. Human as animal, as nascent form. She has always been in awe of the artist who is able to suggest so much through so little.

Standing, she drops the little figure into her coat pocket, but as she walks she finds herself reaching in and folding her hand around it. It feels like a pod or an oversized seed. Funny little thing. It makes her smile already.

A few friends stay by the fire into the night, adding branches for warmth. When they are ready to depart, they pack the remains of the ceremony and clamber up the riverbank to the waiting cars. Amber is last to leave. Before she does, she takes one last look at the scene from the bank. There is nothing left to tell of what happened here but remnant fire, the pulse of embers, a red glow. Before the brilliance of the desert sky, she thinks to herself, *I will remember this forever*, the creature that burned before them tonight. 'I will hold you forever,' she says with no sound, like a whisper or a prayer set upon the night air. She squeezes the small figure in her pocket. She means it of her brother as well as her friend. All this time she had thought grief might be healed if she could only let go. Now, in this moment, she thinks the opposite. You hold your loved ones. You hold your loved ones, and never let go.

This is the same river she came to when her brother died, and she lay in its rushing. It is the first river, in fact, that she saw in flow when she came to the desert. Her first desert rain. She recalls how her friend had said, 'Look, Amber! The river! It's flowing!' as they'd passed on their way out of town. It is difficult to describe what it is to see a landscape transform like this. What you'd always seen as sand, though they called it a river, all at once ribbons of water that merge to become a single swirling body, writhing through the country.

It is the same river, she thought when she arrived today to set up. All the things that had happened here. Birthdays, farewells, fireside gatherings. It'd been a while since last it rained. The sand was no longer smooth and unbroken, as it was when the river had recently drained. People had been here, wild animals. The surface was churned up and choppy.

But there were signs of the river's presence, if you looked. Leavings in the landscape. Bowls scoured out under river red gums, exposing massive roots, now matted with grass and sticks and other debris. It was as if the riverbed held the memory of the river, or the spirit of the river was ever-present. As if the past and present were partners in an endless dance, out of time with each other.

And each time it flows, the landscape is transformed. Each time it flows, the waterholes and soaks are flushed out, the riverbed sculptured anew. It is something Amber has always loved about this country. Its propensity for recalibration. But she had never thought how this might pertain to herself. The time it takes to heal.

THE THINGS THAT ARE
LEFT BEHIND

It is only days since the funeral when Amber hears that the fossil site she'd always hoped to visit with her brother is to open to the public next weekend. This happens only occasionally, and this time she decides to go, without him. She leaves late in the afternoon on Saturday, a week from the funeral, taking the highway north as the sun releases its grip. The day darkens incrementally as she drives, as if small droplets of ink are being added one by one to the mix of land and sky.

By the time she turns onto the dirt road, the sun is gone. Still a pale glaze of light illuminates the country on all sides, silhouetting the stands of mulgas and other trees along the side of the road. The vehicle is dwarfed by the scale of this landscape, like a matchbox car moving through the world of a child. It is difficult not to see the country as indifferent, untouched, it seems, by the tally of our losses. But this same quality gives Amber comfort, a sense of calm. As if, come what may, the country will carry on.

Night comes inevitably. Soon the headlights take over as light-bearers, and small stars appear like pinholes in the blackened sky. The chill of the desert evening pierces through a partially open window and she turns just slightly to wind the handle. It is then that she sees the moon. And she sees that the moon is a crescent, all but new.

In the morning, the group is already trailing down to the fossil pit when Amber arrives at the breakfast shed. She empties the dregs of coffee from a pot and follows, cup in hand. At the pit, twenty or so people gather around one man. Behind him, two or three lie on their sides or crouch in the pit, picking away with scribes and brushes at a dusty bed of bones, packed firmly in the hardened clay. Amber recognises the speaker as the palaeontologist from the museum.

In the pit, a flock of prehistoric birds – bones collided and wings collapsed. Giant flightless birds – *Dromornis stirtoni* – entangled and twisted by the fate of thirst: the final tableau in what the palaeontologist terms 'a mass mortality event'. Tethered to the waterhole by drought, the animals had finally collapsed in the mud, from thirst and exhaustion, as the last water slowly evaporated. When finally the water they yearned for did arrive, it came in the form of a flood that set the carcasses in motion again, tumbling down the waterway, their remains jumbled. It is the final irony that, while a lack of water cost them their lives, it was water that preserved them in this mass grave, cemented in time by clay.

Thylacinus potens, Wakaleo alcootaensis, Baru, Kolopsis torus, Plaisiodon centralis, Palorchestes painei, Pyramios alcootense. Spoken aloud, the classificatory names sound like phrases from a long-forgotten chant as this motley mix of marsupials, birds and crocodiles are drawn from their death beds by tiny brushstrokes and breath, and born again in the daylight glare. Seeing the strange forms emerge, Amber can well imagine how in earlier times dinosaur bones were seen as the remains of mythological creatures, evidence of dragons and other fantastical beasts.

It is difficult to date the site, they are told, in the absence of material suitable for radioactive dating. As he picks away at a protruding pelvis, their guide explains that the assemblage has been dated by comparison to a site of similar age in the south of the country, where one of the same species existed. He talks about the late Miocene: a time when the climate was drying and cooling. When the palaeontologist talks about deep time, Amber's mind reaches, falters and fails. One thousand years is almost imaginable, ten thousand perhaps, but at the mention of seven million, nine million years, she is flailing. He tries to simplify the sums, asks them to place not decades but 'periods' together to arrive at some kind of understanding of an 'epoch' and set time in motion again. But beyond a certain measure, such units of time are intangible. 'Smaller than a period and larger than an age,' he offers.

Amber gives up trying to comprehend time. All she can think about is the brevity of a single life in all of this. It is not much, really, but a small bundle of years. A series of twists and turns and troubles to be negotiated as they appear on the road. And yet how infinite the breadth and depth of each of us. Growing like roots into the soil of the earth, in and around each other.

The man beside her interrupts her thoughts as he passes her a specimen. In her hand the tooth of an ancient mammal that once lived here, preserved in silt, like stone. She turns it in her hand, this precious link to the past. 'Remnants', he calls them. The things that are left behind. Shafts of bone bound together by glue as soon as they are exposed to the air, lest they crumble while being extracted. Pelvises, vertebrae, teeth and splintered skulls, eye sockets scraped bare and empty. At once artefacts, foreign and exotic; at once deeply familiar, for there is a kind of kinship here.

That night she lies awake under a glittering night sky. It is as if the camp is being watched by a thousand wakeful eyes, witnesses to a past that has played itself out on these plains for aeons – a past that remains in relative darkness until scientists find enough reference points to begin a rough sketch. Like the early cartographers, they chart it into being, as they bring more and more evidence to light. Yet such perfect conditions are needed to preserve it that the fossil record contains absences, interruptions to the narrative and whole missing chapters, like those vast regions on early explorers' maps rendered in darkness.

Remnant smoke from the campfire circles, smudges the dark. She turns on her side. In the distance is a broken line of hills whose peaks chart the remains of all that has not been eroded of the ancient ground level. Among them is a fossil hill they visited today. A little more 'recent' than the pit, the hill is dated between five and six million years, another burial site packed firm with the bone fragments of ancient beasts. Tinged in citrine moonlight, the grass plains appear magical. She can well imagine animals at another scale roaming. Against this landscape, she is small.

When finally she sleeps, she dreams of strange beasts. Lion-like figures tangled with giant, long-necked mammals press close. In the morning she peels back the canvas of the swag. The daylight is blinding. She scrapes the ground around her for kindling and makes a fire. It is then that she sees the outline of her boots temporarily etched into the sand. They will be washed away when the next rains come and the water floods this country. Or eroded by the wind. Her presence here will not be recorded, and will remain another absence in the record of time.

Acknowledgements

I wish to acknowledge and thank all of those who have supported me, directly and indirectly, in the writing of this book.

Among those who read the work, in its various incarnations, I would especially like to thank Ute Eberle, Kim Mahood, Michael Cawthorn and Catherine Lewis. And, more recently, dear friends Desdemona Shee, Sue McLeod and Sylvia Purrurle Neale, for the care they took in reading closely, and for their encouragement and reflections. Also thanks to Angela Lynch for her reading of some sections. For providing critique and encouragement at earlier stages of the journey, I thank Peter Bishop, Janet Hutchinson and Arnold Zable.

My heartfelt thanks in particular to Carol Major, who helped me see the work for what it was, who believed in me for its telling, and who offered invaluable guidance at several crossroads.

Special thanks to Terri-ann White for her belief in and commitment to this work. Thanks also to all the staff at UWA Publishing, and especially to my editor, Julian Welch, for the close eye, and for the care taken.

Words cannot capture the gratitude I felt for the gift of a room of my own on several occasions at Varuna, the National Writers' House, in the Blue Mountains, as well as the solidarity and support of staff and fellow writers in residence. For this I thank the Eleanor Dark Foundation and the Northern

Territory Government through Arts NT, who supported some of the time I spent in residence. I would also like to thank Sue McLeod and Peter Yates for offering the solitude of the hut on the hill at a time I needed it most.

Thank you to Rebecca Defina for reviewing the Pitjantjatjara language, and to Yanyi Bandicha and Sam Osborne for their generous assistance with referencing the Pitjantjatjara hymn. Also to Adam Yates at the Museum of Central Australia for checking my memory of the megafauna and fossil beds at the Alcoota Scientific Reserve.

Thank you to Michael, for the many conversations that deepened the work, for being my main sounding board, and for his support, belief and patience in the process of writing. And to Reuben, for his daily offerings of love and insight, and for his unending curiosity and attention to the things of this world.

I write this novella with great respect for the Arrernte people, whose land I live on in Mparntwe/Alice Springs; they have taught me much, and influenced me immeasurably. And I write in honour of the Pitjantjatjara, Ngaanyatjarra and Yankunytjatjara people, with whom I have spent time and worked with over the past twenty years, and whose lands and culture inspired some of this story. I did not write about any person in particular or any one place in order to protect peoples' privacy, but in drawing on my experiences living in Central Australia I hope I have conveyed something of the people and places that are now embedded within me. I feel changed by the privilege of living and working in this country, and I write with gratitude for the generosity and patience shown to me, and for the learning and insight I continue to receive. For their trust, advice and reassurance about writing in this space, I would especially like to thank Lorna Wilson, Yanyi Bandicha and Imitjala Lewis.

Pieces of this novella, in various forms, have appeared elsewhere, including as 'Return to Dust', published in *Island* 126 (2011) and in *Bruno's Song and Other Stories from the Northern Territory* (Northern Territory Writers' Centre, 2011); as 'Coming Back', published in *Island* 131 (2012); as 'The Coming Home Car', published in *Fishtails in the Dust: Writing from the Centre* (Ptilotus Press, 2009); and as 'Sketch of This Day', which won the Poetry Prize at the Northern Territory Literary Awards in 2009 and was published in *Northern Territory Literary Awards 2009* (Northern Territory Government, 2009).

'A Child of the High Seas' extracts are from "L'enfant de la haute mer" by Jules Supervielle © Editions Gallimard 1931, 1958. This translation by Dorothy Baker, first appeared in *Orpheus: A Symposium of the Arts*, volume 1, edited by John Lehmann, London, 1948. Copyright ©1948 by New Directions. Reprinted with permission.

The hymn 'Walkunila Pitalytji Pulka' is a Pitjantjatjara translation of the ancient Christian hymn 'Phos Hilaron', known from John Keble's translation as 'Hail, Gladdening Light'. Senior Pitjantjatjara woman Yanyi Bandicha and others remember this hymn fondly as being sung in Pukatja (Ernabella) at the close of day during mission times, before people dispersed to their wiltja or shepherd's camp. This translation is attributed to the Pitjantjatjara Council, 1978. It appears in *Nyiri Inmatjara Lutheran Uwankaraku* (Pitjantjatjara Lutheran Hymnal), published by Finke River Mission of the Lutheran Church of Australia, Inc., 2010.

Lyrics from 'Prisoner' by the Lajamanu Teenage Band are used with the kind permission of CAAMA Music; see www.caamamusic.com.au/catalogue/prisoner.

Glossary

Pitjantjatjara is a Western Desert language, widely spoken in Central Australia. Pitjantjatjara words used in this book conform to the spellings given in *Pitjantjatjara/Yankunytjatjara to English Dictionary* (revised second edition), compiled by Cliff Goddard and updated by Rebecca Defina (IAD Press, Alice Springs, 2020). The English translations below are confined to the words' intended meaning in the narrative.

ai (exclam)	huh? What?! Indicates surprise, often combined with indignation or incredulity
ananyi (v)	go somewhere, travel, move along
ila (adj/adv)	near, close
ilaringanyi (v)	become close, near, draw near
kapaṯi (n)	cup of tea (from English)
kapi (n)	water
kulini (v)	listen to, heed; think about, consider
kungka (n)	woman (mostly younger woman)
kunmaṉara (n)	substitute name used when the name of a person is the same as, or sounds like, the name of someone recently deceased
kutju (adj/adv)	1. one 2. on its own, single, alone
kutjupa (adj/n)	other, another, a different one
maḻpa (n)	companion, company, friend
mamu (n)	harmful spirit being, spirit-monster, 'devil' animal

mina (n)	nest, of bird or rodent
mingkul(pa) (n)	wild tobaccos, pituri. The dried leaves are powdered and mixed with the ashes of certain plants and chewed
mulapa (adv)	true, real
ngaltutjara (n/excl)	someone deserving pity, sympathy or compassion; 'poor thing!'
ngangkari (n)	healer, traditional doctor
ngapari (n)	sweet crusty lerp scales found on leaves of gum trees
ngura (n)	camp, home, place where people are staying, or could stay
nyangatja (adv)	here, right here
nyaratja (dem adv)	over there
palya (adj)	good, fine
punu (n)	1. living/growing tree or bush 2. piece of wood, stick, cut-off branches
rama-rama (adj)	(from 'rama') mad, crazy, not responsible for one's actions
tili (n)	flame, light
tjitji (n)	child, kid
tjiwa (n)	1. lower flat grindstone 2. any smooth flat rock or stone
tjuka (n)	sugar (from English)
ultu (adj)	empty
uwa	yes
walpa (n)	wind
walpa pulka (n)	a strong wind
wampa (excl)	'I wouldn't know', 'search me', 'how would I know?'
wanti (v)	leave it (alone)

wiltja (n)   1. shade 2. shade shelter, wurlie, bush hut (note: the plural form is anglicised and does not exist in Pitjantjatjara language)

wiṟu (adj)   great, lovely, fine, nice

wiya (excl/n/adj)   1. no 2. nothing, none, no

yaaltji (adv)   where?